£10
SIGNED
BY
AUTHOR

CW01084553

CHINK OF MEDALS

To Glan Morgan who
practices Service Before Self

Llewellyn Edwards.

CHINK OF MEDALS

Llewellyn Edwards

The Book Guild Ltd.
Sussex, England

The Book Guild Limited
Temple House
25 High Street
Lewes, Sussex

First published 1991
© Llewellyn Edwards 1991

Set in Baskerville

Typesetting by Unit Eleven Typeset
Burgess Hill, Sussex

Printed in Great Britain by
Antony Rowe Ltd
Chippenham, Wiltshire

British Library Cataloguing in Publication Data
Edwards Llewellyn
Chink of medals
I. Title
823.914 [F]

ISBN 0 86332 625 0

CONTENTS

THE PARADE	7		**THE PARADE**	89
Llewellyn	9		*Owen*	90
THE PARADE	24		**THE PARADE**	97
Glenys	25		*Jean*	98
THE PARADE	30		**THE PARADE**	102
Dad	32		*Gareth*	103
THE PARADE	40		**THE PARADE**	109
Mam	41		*Ann*	110
THE PARADE	48		**THE PARADE**	118
Andrew	49		*John*	119
THE PARADE	58		**THE PARADE**	124
Megan	59		*Catherine*	125
THE PARADE	63		**THE PARADE**	135
Avril	64		*Gwen*	136
THE PARADE	70		**THE PARADE**	140
Ivor	71		*Rhys*	141
THE PARADE	75		**THE PARADE**	150
Sian	76		*Epigraph*	151
THE PARADE	83		*The Gulf War*	153
Phillip	84			

---

*In memory of my Dad and brothers
including all who made the supreme
sacrifice during the First and
Second World Wars or after their
return to their families*

CHINK OF MEDALS

TO DAD

*Old Soldiers do die but to
Llewellyn never fade away.*

THE PARADE

The November morning was cold and sunny as Llewellyn and his brother-in-law Phillip walked towards the car park used as a parade ground to form up for the British Legion Remembrance Sunday Parade and Service. They left their wives Glenys, and Sian to make their own way to the Cenotaph. The expressions on the faces of Llewellyn and Phillip showed they appreciated the significance of the occasion, and coupled with their own thoughts and memories of the Remembrance.

Contingents of the Royal Air Force, Army, Royal Navy, Cadets, Guides, Scouts, and other voluntary organisations were walking around trying to find their place in the order of the parade. Parents of the younger elements were attempting to pacify them as they tried to keep them in groups, but at times it seemed they were at the point of disaster. There were considerable signs of activity amongst the ex-service personnel as the parade ground started to fill up and an atmosphere of expectation of the occasion built up. Old friends and comrades looked out for each other. A quick wave of acknowledgement as they walked towards each other with handshakes all round, and a hint of nervous laughter.

Over the far corner of the parade ground the military band was making final preparations for the 'Get On Parade'. Senior military personnel and the town representatives were waiting for the Mayor and his party to arrive. The detached expressions shown on their faces were based on past knowledge that everything would right itself before the parade formed up.

The lone ex-serviceman could be seen looking for his friends, and/or contingent and one could by this time feel the genuine comradeship generating itself amongst all the groups waiting on the parade ground. The glitter reflecting from the medals worn on parade suggested some of them had been up half the previous night polishing them.

The RSM could be seen obtaining last minute instructions from the Officer commanding the parade, then he saluted him and marched towards the main contingents and attempted to arrange the order of precedence of the parade, and the individual asked to join a contingent of their own choice. The RSM called out for 'Right Markers' from each contingent to form up on parade as per his instructions.

The mood of all attending the parade seemed to change, and this helped the parents of the younger elements in trying to form up into a resemblance of order. In a loud voice the RSM could be heard saying, 'Get On Parade'. They lined up to their appropriate right marker. The RSM with a smile said, 'Lets show the Regulars how it is done.' The ex-servicemen with the discipline ingrained into them after many years training instinctively took over.

After the initial confusion which takes place for the first few seconds or so the parade took on the semblance of order. The RSM satisfied all queries, and waited for the Officer commanding the parade to bring them to attention. He looked at the parade and saw they had formed into recognisable patterns, and that they were waiting with anticipation for the order 'Parade Parade Shun'. There was a pause between the first and second word 'parade' there was an instant straightening of backs, and with the word 'shun' the almost single clatter of feet and then complete silence from the parade, and from those watching the parade.

At that moment Llewellyn looked down at the British Legion wreath in his left hand, and thought of the names on the card attached to the wreath. He remembered each name as part of the family he belonged to. Llewellyn saw Phillip looking at him, and asked what was wrong, but Llewellyn looked straight ahead, and thought back.

MAM RHYS SAID:

'LLEWELLYN IS THE BRAINY ONE.'

MAM RHYS SAID:

'Llewellyn is the Brainy One.'

LLEWELLYN EDWARDS looked back over many years, and remembered when he first knew Rhys was his brother. Rhys being the younger, their Mam said it was Llewellyn's job to look after him. They would go to school together, and neither of them had any difficulties in learning or taking part in the school sports.

Looking after Rhys was a source of contention amongst others from both their classes. During playtime they sometimes became the butt of remarks made to them and it usually ended up in a fight, and if reported meant a visit to the headmaster. The culprits were punished but Rhys, being younger, would only be reprimanded by him. Their brother Gareth was in a class between Llewellyn and Rhys, and because he was so short for his age got himself into trouble with the other boys but coped without the need of help from them.

It seemed as though Llewellyn and Rhys would have to defend themselves for the duration of their school days. At first it was Llewellyn who had to do most of the fighting, but that's what brothers and families are for, and brought about by a closeness many others envied. Llewellyn always had bumps and bruises because of his involvement with the boys at school, and regularly received a few sharp words and a clip from his mam to remind him to look after Gareth and Rhys.

John, who was the oldest and a few classes ahead of Llewellyn, was never asked to look after his younger brothers. Llewellyn would often wonder why, but it was only later in life did he realise the reason why and made him think his mam was wiser than given credit for.

In the evenings after school, and at the weekend Llewellyn would go about with the gang, but Rhys was not included. However, he would follow at a safe distance. If spotted he would pretend to run away. Sometimes one of the gang would hide and wait until Rhys was near enough and if Rhys was caught it would usually start a fight, and naturally once Rhys was involved Llewellyn would side with him against the rest of the gang. Finally a truce was called and from then on he would be allowed to walk with them without any involvement with what the rest of the gang were doing.

Eventually Rhys won them over and became a full member. Shortly afterwards Gareth joined and with the three of them they had no trouble from the rest of the gang. They became known as the 'Inseparable Brothers'.

As they grew older Llewellyn began to notice a change in Rhys, not easy to define. Also the first signs of leadership qualities were noticeable to the family and others. Later it helped to save his life and others under his command. Something else, less obvious and tangible and which could be more frightening became evident and Llewellyn felt a shiver down his back, but it was a long time before the features he saw in Rhys were remembered by Llewellyn. He thought of telling his mam, but felt she already knew.

Llewellyn and Rhys successfully completed their school examinations and Llewellyn through the help of his dad started work as an apprentice at the colliery he worked at. It would be a few years before Rhys could leave school. Llewellyn had little time for going around with the boys as apart from being tired he had enrolled at the technical college for evening classes and homework kept him busy most nights. However, Sunday was a day with family.

A regular Saturday night out with other apprentices was a must, and having pocket-money enabled him to buy fruit and monkey-nuts at the market which he would take home to share with the family. The girls would be chatted up, and the night finishing up with chips and a hot pie with a bottle of lemonade. The walk home was about two miles, and as he neared his house his younger brothers would be looking out of the bedroom window for him and the usual bag of fruit and monkey nuts were handed over to their delight.

During the few years before Rhys left school Gareth had the task of looking after him. It must have been difficult as he was at least six inches shorter than Rhys, but it made no difference to Gareth as he was not afraid to tackle anyone, irrespective of size, when it involved his brothers. When Gareth left school his dad was able to get him started as an apprentice electrician locally. Gareth was certainly pleased with his new job.

A year later Rhys started work at the same colliery as Llewellyn. His mam bought him a new cycle so they were able to go to work together. It was like old times, but as Llewellyn was already two years into his apprenticeship they saw little of each other during their time at work. Two other apprentices including Llewellyn and his brother would travel to work each morning. They would meet outside their mam's house. They did this for three years. In the winter they were all so cold when they arrived at the colliery that they would make straight for the warm boilerhouse to warm themselves. Their hands were so cold they almost cried with the pain when they started to thaw out.

The last two miles of the journey to work was a long uphill ride and whenever the opportunity arose they would hold on to the back end of the coach taking miners to work and have a free tow up the hill. Usually, as well as the one hanging on to the coach one of them would hold on to the other. On reflection it was pretty dangerous and proved to be shortly afterwards. Llewellyn on one occasion was hanging on to the coach when the front wheel of the cycle hit a pothole. He said he remembered the side of his face hitting the newly tarred road without any pain, and the next thing was waking up in the first-aid room of the colliery, his face covered in lacerations and in considerable pain. He was off work for two weeks. He never hung on the back of a coach again.

During the years before the start of the war in 1939 there were rumours of Germans invading those countries next to her borders, usually without any warning. We were too young or ill-informed to understand this, but developed a hatred for Germans, or anything German. All this tension resulted in a regiment of infantry troops being called up and sent to our village. They were billeted in the church hall and other empty buildings all around the village. The officers stayed at the local houses. There certainly was some fierce competition amongst the better off women in the village to billet the officers.

The troops were an attraction to the local and girls from the nearby town of Neath. When dances were held to entertain the troops it would lead to the occasional fight with the local boys over the girls. It was strange we would want to fight amongst ourselves and at the same time the Germans were invading other countries. Is this how wars start or is it more obvious? Once the novelty of having troops wore off the community made the troops most welcome. They would be invited to tea on Sunday. Some of the troops started courting, and others married the local girls. Some were unlucky, and left with babies on the way. When the crisis was over the troops left the village. There were tears from the girls and the friendships made during their stay would be missed.

The visit of the troops instilled in the locals a sense of patriotism in the brothers who before the start of the Second World War joined the Territorial Army. There was a good choice of regiments including the Royal Air Force. Their mam and dad were proud of them, but were worried they all chose a 'Fighting Regiment'. They enjoyed drill night and were proud to wear their uniforms. The drill hall was staffed by permanent soldiers called Staff Sergeants. They knew their jobs and were helpful at all times. Looking back to the war years it is as well to remember that without their dedication many of those they trained so well would not be here now. They were marvellous times and in the company of other volunteers, for the first time the brothers felt themselves growing up. At home after attending the drill hall for training there would be mild disagreements amongst the brothers as to who was the best soldier but it never went any further than that as they respected each other too much. They still had their Saturday night out, but less and less because of the demands of the TA. The mood of the country was changing, and so did their sense of responsibility and outlook.

The highlight of their training was the two weeks' annual camp when they were trained by regular soldiers, and paid as regulars. (It is worth remembering that statutory and paid holidays were the exception, unless Sunday School trips to the seaside were included.) The months up to September seemed long but Llewellyn was kept busy as apart from TA training he also attended the technical college for two evenings per week. With the examinations due in June and knowing good results would help with promotion it was an added incentive. However, he need not have worried because he passed all the subjects with a good pass mark. He said he can still remember after many years, and it would be said without fail by Rhys to his mam, 'Llewellyn Is The Brainy One.'

Even though the brothers were going to TA camp at different times they spent most evenings preparing their kit, which included polishing buttons and cap badges, also plenty of blancoing and buffing. They had unofficial competitions to see who was the smartest. Their mam and dad would act as judges. They would pick out individual points for each of their sons, but never declare an outright winner. This judgement satisfied them all.

They went to TA camp at different times, and all were given the same loving goodbye from their mam and dad who would watch them from the front door as they walked to the bus-stop carrying their rifle, kitbag, and full kit. The weather for Llewellyn's two weeks' camp was the best of the summer. He trained hard and was soon promoted to lance-corporal. The time went very quickly. He made lots of new friends, and they went to the Naafi and cinema at the barracks of the regular soldiers. There was initially some resentment with his friends when he was promoted, but it was soon forgotten and all back to being the best of mates in B Squadron.

On the Friday night before they left on the Saturday morning the Colonel of the Regiment spoke to them all as he stood on a large wooden packing case, and asked them all to gather round in a circle. He told all of them how proud he was, and how well the regiment had integrated with the regular soldiers, and in his conversation with the regular officers they had nothing but praise for them. The colonels's voice took on a more serious note as he mentioned the invasion of Austria and Czechoslovakia with the probable invasion of Poland, and it would be more than likely the regiment would be mobilised within the next few weeks. They were a sombre lot on their return home on the Saturday and were beginning to realise the seriousness of the situation.

Llewellyn's brothers went to TA camp either before or after him, and never saw them again until after the war, and in one instance never saw Gareth again. Some of the brothers were stationed near enough to come home for week-ends. They were all put up in houses, chapels, old buildings, and even a prison.

Llewellyn was called up on Friday 1 September 1939, but was sent home and told to report the next morning. It was utter chaos with nobody knowing what to do. Llewellyn was in B Squadron. There were no meals laid on so everybody drifted into local cafes for something to eat. Eventually everybody was told there would be a medical inspection at 14.00 hrs. The regiment lined up in three columns/open order, and told to drop their trousers and raise their battledress jacket and shirt. The medical officer walked along each column and occasionally stopped and asked a question, or tentatively took a closer look using his cane, but he certainly did not waste time and it was over very quickly. (It was not known whether he missed any one-armed, or one-legged soldier on his rounds.)

Another queue was formed to sign for the £5 mobilisation money and be sworn in. They were all now members of HM Armed Forces. Llewellyn would now receive fourteen shillings per week (70p). Like his brothers, Llewellyn made an allocation of five shillings per week to his parents.

They were anxious times for their mam and dad. One day they had four sons at home and then they were all in the army. They were left with three young children. Their dad knew all about war as he served in the First World War and taken a prisoner of war in 1917.

Llewellyn was put on guard at a large docks, and in December given embarkation leave for Egypt. He was the only one of the brothers in the army to be home for Xmas. During his leave he met some of the gang who were on leave from the British Expeditionary Forces (BEF) in France. They met most evenings either at the local or retraced the walks they had had before the war started. But it was not the time or place to look back and they were glad when the leave was over and they could return to their regiments.

The war years between 1939 and 1946 on looking back seemed to have gone like a flash but if anybody had said in 1939 the war would last until 1945 no one would have believed them. Llewellyn remembered all the talk about the Germans only having cardboard tanks and how the war would be over by Xmas 1939. It would have been a not so nice thought if up against a squadron on German Panzer 11 or King Tiger tanks as they were certainly not made of cardboard. It's surprising how soon one changes from being an atheist to a quickly found deity to pray to when a few Tiger tanks are bearing down towards you.

Llewellyn was demobbed in January 1946. He was the first of the brothers and it was a wonderful day. He was sent to the demob centre at Guildford, and as the paperwork was being completed he went around and at the end of a large building was kitted out from head to foot. The selection was of his own choice and there were experts at hand to measure and advise if required. All the items were packed in a specially made cardboard box, a railway warrant issued together with relevant discharge paperwork. Outside the demob centre there were men, usually called spivs offering up to £20 for all the contents of the box and there was no lack of sellers.

Llewellyn had in late 1944 married Glenys. They first met in 1938 when he was visiting his mam at the local hospital where she was training for her SRN. They saw little of each other in 1939 because of his TA training and night school. They met for a few hours in January 1940 and the next time they met was in 1944. With what money they were both able to save they put a deposit down for a house built in 1939. It cost them £950. (In 1939 it cost £175.)

He decided not to go back to the colliery, and started work with a local civil engineering firm dismantling anti-blast steelwork and brickwork fitted around petrol storage tanks and removing steel pipework which was resited after alterations. Petrol would then be repumped from the refinery into the same storage tanks. It was a welcome change from colliery work for Llewellyn.

Shortly afterwards John and Rhys returned home from overseas and demobbed. Both had changed almost to the point that they were hardly recognizable and looked like old men, with Rhys looking the older. They went from being very young men in 1939 to men who showed their war on their faces. John never returned to colliery work and quickly found a suitable job, but he was never well enough for heavy work. He would not complain, but it was evident he would not again be a well man. Looking at him it could be wondered what he had to do for his 'Mention In Despatches' in Italy.

Rhys, like the other brothers, did not return to colliery work, and it was sometime before he was able to start any form of work. He served in Burma and, remembering how tall he was, now looked like a little old man. He had lost the smart spring in his step but his brothers knew it was the last thing he wanted to be reminded of and that he would not thank anyone for doing so. All the fears for Rhys was lost with the wonderful smile only he of all the family had. Llewellyn could do no more than shake off his most inner thoughts and remembered what his mam said to him many years ago – that he should look after him. Llewellyn wondered if this was now or is it still to come, and for the first time in his life he felt frightened as to what would happen. Llewellyn knew he would protect him with his own life if necessary, but could also think what would be required of him when the time came.

Rhys started work in the maintenance department of a large transport firm, and slowly but surely there was some return in health. Owen by this time had left them to do his National Service in the Royal Air Force. The family were equally as proud of him as the other sons. He was the first one not to chose the Army. Gareth was killed on the beach-head at Arromanches in Normandy in June 1944 and Llewellyn never saw him from the time they were all called up in 1939, but to him his face is as clear and fresh in his mind as all those years ago.

Llewellyn settled down to home life and Glenys started work as a staff nurse at the small British Legion hospital. It was the first time in a long time they felt secure as a family after being separated during the war. At least their love had been surely tested. Llewellyn never neglected to call and see his mam and dad and regularly was part of the Saturday night out all the family had every other week. It seemed as though they needed something positive to keep them together after they were all apart for so long. Their mam and dad for the first time were able to settle down within the family and not have to worry every time they heard the war news on the radio. Their dad looked a lot better as he never properly recovered from the effects of the trenches and his time as a prisoner of war in the First World War.

Llewellyn's sister Sian and brother Andrew were now in their teens. During the war a second daughter was born, and became the favourite of all the family. As a child she was very pretty. Avril as she was called easily became frightened and nervous and would cry without warning. Glenys put it down to the lack of family life as the family were separated for such a long period.

Llewellyn enrolled for night classes in order to complete his ONC in mechanical engineering. After discussion with the headmaster it was agreed he would not have to start from the beginning, but take up from when he finished in 1939. It was a hard slog, and even trying to remember the simplest of formulae was difficult. The lecturer of the course was helpful, and whenever possible took extra time with him so he could keep up with the class.

Glenys gave him all the help she could as her favourite subject was maths, but he thought he would never get through the course. However, in the end perseverance paid off and he completed the ONC with a good pass mark. He was now able to apply for a better qualified position. He eventually joined the planning department as a planning engineer. The hours were shorter and with a higher salary and the work was hard but he was able to make a success of his new position and was considering taking the higher national diploma, but felt it would not be fair to Glenys so decided to leave it for another year.

During this time Owen had completed his National Service and returned to work. Owen married shortly afterwards, but not before an interrupted courtship. Probably they were both testing their love for each other. The wedding was held at St John's church with a reception afterwards at her parents' home. The house was packed, with plenty to eat and drink. A buffet was laid on in the evening at The Crown Hotel. Again it was packed with the families and all their friends. The piano set the scene for everyone to have a good time. Turns were given by Glenys, Rhys, and Owen plus anyone who felt like singing.

By this time Glenys and Llewellyn had put a deposit on a detached house a few miles from the village.

Within what seemed to be a short time Rhys and Gwen were getting married. It was a warm and sunny day so the women were able to dress up. Llewellyn was best man which kept him busy all the afternoon. The reception was held at the village hall, all the families providing the food and drink with friends waiting on the tables. The men had the responsibility of getting the drinks and so soon after the war 'shorts' were difficult to come by. All the dishes, cutlery, and glasses were provided by the family, and all the tables laid out before they could attend the wedding ceremony. The buttonholes were handed out to the families and guests as they entered the church. All these activities helped to create the right

17

atmosphere for the occasion.

Wedding presents were a problem as there were shortages, so it was mostly money they were given and it was more than welcome. After the wedding ceremony most of the guests other than the bride and groom would have to walk from the church to the reception. Everyone enjoyed the wedding breakfast and the buffet arranged for the evening. Rhys and Gwen left the buffet early as they were booked into one of the hotels for a week-end honeymoon.

It must be a wedding fever because all too soon afterwards Sian and Phillip decided to marry, and within a short space of time Andrew and Megan were married.

By this time Llewellyn was asked to take on the position of junior manager at one of their other factories. It was an offer he could not refuse, but it would mean moving. The family were happy for the promotion and tried to hide their disappointment at leaving the village. Llewellyn restarted night school the following September, taking economics, commerce and English. It took him two years to complete the course. The homework took up a lot of time and he had to use his lunch-time and weekends.

Glenys in the meanwhile had accepted a post as Theatre sister. Between the two of them they had little time together and both welcomed the family Saturday night out.

They had their first holiday and went down to Bournemouth. The weather was great. On their return they decided to buy a second-hand car. Both took driving lessons and Glenys passed her test first time so she used the car for travelling to work. She became an excellent driver never losing her temper and always considerate to other road users. She was always a better driver than Llewellyn, but never said so to him.

John by this time had emigrated to Australia. He stayed a few days with Llewellyn before he left. He had changed considerably since the war. He certainly was not a well man and had gone downhill in the short time from leaving the army. He became nervous with little colour in his face. Who was going to take care of him? Perhaps the Scots girl he met when visiting his general.

Llewellyn and John had a few wonderful days together and talked about old times. John never missed the occasion to slightly exaggerate the point, but had a smile when he was in that mood. When you looked hard enough you could see the man behind the face and it was the same one who won an award for bravery.

Llewellyn went with him when he boarded his ship. It was an emotional goodbye. The ship took a long time to go out of sight. Llewellyn waited until there was nothing further to see. The journey home seemed long and tedious and was full of thoughts. He was glad when he saw Glenys looking through the window when he drew up. Rhys also waited with Glenys. Llewellyn could not look at him because he seemed to be racked with pain. Llewellyn at that moment wished he could share or even take the pain from him. All he could say under his breath was, 'Rhys, Rhys how can you be helped?'

They went out for a drink, but neither of them enjoyed it so they did not stay long. Llewellyn drove him home. He had a very uneasy few days and thought it is as well we are not gifted to peek into the future.

Turning to prayer gives some satisfaction, but it is only in war time is it forced home to one by sheer panic in battle when the need for moral support of a higher being is of paramount importance. On the other hand, praying should not be like frozen food which adverts say are cheap, quick and convenient.

On the following Sunday they had one of those high teas which reminded them of the Sunday teas with the family before the war when the table was loaded with cooked meat, salads, tinned fruit, custard, cream, home-made teisen lap, and plates of fresh bread and butter. What halcyon days they were. When tea was over everybody was too full to move, but still able to drink a few bottles of beer. To round off the evening their dad would play the piano and they would all give a song or join in with the singing.

Glenys could not stop thinking about Rhys and as her concern would show on her face it was to her he would confide, knowing she understood what kept him in constant pain. The doctor would always bring Glenys into the conversation after he visited Rhys.

Things returned to normal at home and they regularly had letters from John. Their dad had the opportunity to buy the house he was renting, but did not feel he should lay out so much money. When Llewellyn offered to help with the repayments it was all settled. It proved to be a worthwhile investment for them when he had to finish work many years after. The asking price was £700 for a large semi-detached house.

Eventually, with Glenys having a sister living a few miles away and her husband David being a good friend of Rhys, they became almost part of the family and included the Saturday night family night out as theirs as well.

Llewellyn's youngest sister Avril by this time had grown into a very pretty teenager with her mam and dad having to put up with a regular procession of young boys hanging about outside the house hoping to date her. She was shy and lacked self-confidence in their company. This was put down to most of the older members being away during the war during her formative years and her mam and dad both working. Eventually a young man by the name of Ivor started dating her. He had only recently completed his National Service with the South Wales Borderers an infantry regiment known for their outstanding war record, and the VCs won in the Zulu War.

Ivor started work with a firm of industrial painters as a labourer and after a few months was promoted to 'rough painter'.

Theirs was a problematic courtship from the beginning with their insistence on keeping to themselves and an aura of secrecy which prevented the family either individually or collectively from getting to know Ivor. It was most strange as Avril was part of such an open family.

The family went to their wedding and on that particular day it was very cold, with stormy winds. Llewellyn wondered how their dad could afford such an expensive reception and a lavish selection of drinks. They left before the reception was finished in order to leave for the airport for their honeymoon in Spain. The family had booked a room for the evening with a buffet and, most surprising, Ivor's family attended. When it was all over they thanked Avril's dad and said how they enjoyed the buffet and evening.

Llewellyn's mam and dad spent their holidays every year with him and Glenys. It was something they always looked forward to and the four of them would go on trips most days including a day at Llanwrtyd Wells. Dad would show them the place where he spent most of his summer holidays as a child. On one occasion he took them into the building where the spring water was and offered them a cup of the water. It tasted awful, but he drank it as though it was lemonade.

Their dad would often come down on the spur of the moment and Glenys would find him sitting on the backdoor step waiting for her. Both of them were always at ease with Glenys and Llewellyn. Then dad would finish up the holidays with a meal out on the Friday night. It was their way of thanking them. On the Saturday they would be driven to the main line station for their train, and Rhys would be waiting for them and drive them home.

On the last holiday when they both came down their dad decided to ask Llewellyn to come out on his own. This was not usual and Llewellyn wondered why. During the evening his dad said to him that he hoped he would look after his mam if anything was to happen to him. A month after their dad died.

Llewellyn joined the local bowls club, and took part in the Friday evening practice match, which included a silver spoon competion in which the pair with the highest score received a silver spoon each. Llewellyn gave his spoon to the first born of his brothers and sisters. Matches against other teams were held every Saturday throughout the summer, the venue alternating each week.

Glenys had been promoted to deputy matron and every other week-end would be on duty. This meant Llewellyn fending for himself. He became a very good cook. Llewellyn again had the opportunity to change jobs. This time it was with a firm further away from the village, as a manager in charge of production. The move meant a change of houses. This time it enabled them to buy a large bungalow with a reasonably large plot of land.

Coupled with the move Glenys gave in her notice and decided once they had moved she would concentrate on decorating the bungalow and organising the garden. When she did return to work it was as a relief district nurse in Swansea. She enjoyed the change of work and would always praise the Swansea people because of their kindness towards her.

Glenys would say that as she did the rounds relatives of the patients would look out for her and have a cup of tea ready as she walked into the house.

John and Catherine with their family came over from Australia for a holiday, and shared the time between visiting Scotland and the family. John had met Catherine on a visit to Scotland to see his old general. Catherine lived in the same village as the general. She went out to Australia after John and they were married soon after she arrived.

When John and his family stayed with him he loaned John his car. Llewellyn thought John looked tired and ill, but did not mention this to either Catherine or John. It seemed he did not want to go anywhere in particular and was contented to go for short walks and to the pub for an hour in the evening. Catherine would watch over John like a mother hen. It could be seen they were very much in love.

Catherine and John with the children returned to Scotland for the last few days of their holiday. On their return to Australia Catherine told John how unhappy she was living in Australia and could they return to Scotland to live? Within a few days they decided to sell up as quickly as possible. John died a few days before they left for Scotland.

After their dad died Mam lived on her own, and seemed contented. However, Andrew called every day on his way home from work. Sian and Avril between them gave the house a good clean through every week and made sure the bills were paid. Also they would do the main shopping. Most Sundays and by arrangement one of the family would pick her up and she would have lunch and tea with them. They always made sure she was back home before it was dark. She enjoyed watching TV, but did not like too many visitors. It was too much for her to cope with.

Andrew and Megan made it their job to look after the garden and all the odd jobs including painting the house. Many volunteered but never turned up so it was always left to Andrew.

In spite of the brothers and sisters trying to keep the families together they were fragmented as they moved further away. There was a short period when Rhys was ill and they all made the extra effort to visit him in hospital. Rhys died shortly afterwards.

Their mam never got over the death of Rhys. It seemed as though the losing of three sons and a husband over a short

22

period of time was too much. Their mam eventually asked Sian and Phillip if she could live with them. They never hesitated in saying yes. The house was sold and most of her furniture shared either by consent, or taken without the knowledge of others. The money from the sale was invested and their mam was with her new family in a warm house, her favourite chair, and the television whenever she wanted it.

Llewellyn often asked himself would it not have been better if their dad had not returned from France and saved all the heartache, or is it all part of a greater plan which would only in the end be revealed when the purpose is understood? Llewellyn for no reason thought of the time when he was preparing to take his exams and Glenys telling him to read the questions carefully before writing down the answers.

MAM RHYS SAID:

'LLEWELLYN IS THE BRAINY ONE.'

THE PARADE

Philip nudged Llewellyn as he stood to attention on the Remembrance Sunday Parade and Service, and thought for a few seconds Llewellyn appeared to be in another world, as if he wanted someone to carry the burden which showed on his face. The Parade waited in silence with all eyes facing front to participate in the next command. The RSM marched to the head of the parade and all attending watched until he was in position. The Officer commanding the parade shouted the next command loud enough for all to hear:

'THE PARADE WILL MARCH TO THE CENOTAPH IN COLUMN OF ROUTE'
'MOVE TO THE RIGHT IN COLUMN'
'BY THE LEFT QUICK MARCH'

The band started to play a well-known marching tune, Sons of the Brave, and the parade was on its way. It was long, first with the band, followed by the standard bearers of all the associations, with the Royal British Legion contingent, followed in order of precedence by the other contingents. Above the sound of the band and those marching you could hear the chink of medals as they were disturbed by the movement of the marching. They marched towards the Cenotaph with heads high and arms swinging. Llewellyn could see Glenys trying to take his photograph.

'PARADE' shouted the Commanding Officer *'MARK TIME'*.

As Llewellyn marked time it was as if he was miles away and thinking.

GLENYS SAID TO LLEWELLYN,

'IT IS EASY IF YOU READ THE QUESTION CAREFULLY.'

24

GLENYS SAID TO LLEWELLYN,

'It is easy if you read the question carefully.'

GLENYS. When Llewellyn first met Glenys it was at the local hospital and her first words were, 'No more than two visitors to a bed!' When he eventually plucked up the courage to ask for a date she said yes, and it was the start of a wonderful life together. Looking back, Llewellyn knew she was something special, with a rare and endearing quality and a personality that made one stop and take a second look. Her choice to become a nurse could not be more vocational, with her natural care for those who were sick.

Glenys was one of a large family who lived at the top of the valley and about twenty miles from Llewellyn's village. Her father and brothers worked in the colliery at the end of their road and her sister worked in the colliery wages' office. They were a well respected and God-fearing family. Their mam was an active member of the village with voluntary work and she would always help others in trouble. One could see where Glenys had her kind ways from and why she trained to be a nurse. Glenys had a very fine bone structure and her good looks were naturally Welsh with reddish curly hair which was the envy of all the other nurses. Her fiery eyes and stature was her dad's contribution. He was from Dyfed and her mam from Powis and spoke Welsh. Her mam and dad had a hard life with never enough money to go around without a struggle and the only work was down the pit, with no work for women.

Glenys was very intelligent and passed exams easily. She attended grammar school at eleven years of age and took part in most of the school activities. Her favourite was playing hockey and became captain of the team. She was also an above average tennis player, but her real interest was in the classroom as she had the natural ability to learn and to absorb all knowledge she was taught or read. Most important was her gift to understand without the need to have things explained to her more than once by the teacher. Other class members would seek her out to explain it to them. Her favourite sub-jects were maths, biology, French, Welsh and Latin, and she always had top marks. The headmaster asked her to sit the Oxford entrance exam and consider a medical career, but she said it was nursing she wanted, but would consider a medical degree afterwards. However, the reason she would not discuss was not wanting to impose on her family. Her local doctor intervened to ask her to reconsider, but until she passed her SRN finals she could not be persuaded.

It took longer than expected to complete her training because of an illness that lasted nearly twelve months before she recovered sufficiently to restart her training. However, Glenys did not fully recover from her illness again, but put it all behind her and decided to concentrate on her nursing car-eer. Glenys quickly made her mark in hospital because of her dedication to nursing people, her kindness and tolerance with the older folks and her ability to be part of the hospital staff, but for all that she would not be put upon, or taken advantage of by anyone and would quickly and firmly tell the person involved, often to the person's surprise. She was put in charge of the military wing of the hospital and nursed repatriated ser-vice personnel who had been wounded overseas.

By this time Llewellyn had been posted overseas and did not see her for nearly four years. She had long qualified. She would say the final pattern of the cycle of war are the woun-ded, not necessarily their wounded bodies but their minds. To the nursing staff their reward was the recovery to health of the patient or, if the suffering was too much, then the eventual demise. Contrary to what some may believe, the hospital staff inwardly mourn the death of service personnel and other patients as deeply as relatives and fight hard to keep them alive.

Gareth and Rhys saw Glenys on their leaves until they were eventually posted overseas, and would say to her, 'We will look after you while Llewellyn is away.' In the end they were all posted overseas.

26

When Llewellyn returned from overseas Glenys and he decided to get married. It was over four years since they last saw each other. It was an austere wedding with few or no presents because there was little to buy. It was difficult to buy clothes and usual to borrow a wedding dress from one of the family. The reception was modest, limited to relatives and close friends. It was held at Gleny's house. Fortunately the best man was on leave from the Navy. They all enjoyed the reception.

Llewellyn was on a seventy-two hours pass for the wedding. However, he was able to leave the camp the night before and travel down to Wales without being asked by the military police to show his leave pass. Llewellyn eventually found a flat near the camp and sent for Glenys. She was able to obtain a nursing appointment at the British Legion hospital in Petersfield. The people in Petersfield and the surrounding area were marvellous to the hospital staff. Glenys would come home with eggs, a rabbit, and often a chicken from the local farmers. Nothing was too much trouble to make life easier for the staff.

Glenys and Llewellyn would be invited to their homes for a meal. On Sunday he would be invited by the matron for lunch, and Xmas lunch was a must. In the summer Glenys and Llewellyn would hire a boat for a row on the lake. They would stop in the middle. Glenys would have a nap and Llewellyn would read one of the books loaned to him by the hospital Sister. One day he was reading a new book from the sister and Glenys put it on her lap as Llewellyn rowed the boat. Suddenly he slipped on the oars made the boat rock and the book fell off her lap into the water. It took ages to fish it out and by then it was soaked right through. Glenys told Llewellyn she had never heard so many swear words in her life after the book fell into the water.

After the book was recovered he tried to dry it out, but it started to swell out and was twice as thick as a new book. Glenys tried to buy a new copy, but they were not available. Llewellyn took the book to the printing section at the camp. They pressed every page to reduce the thickness. There was some improvement, but it certainly did not look like a new book. Glenys returned the book to sister with an apology from Llewelyn and the offer to pay for the cost of the book, but sister said no as the book was a present from her younger brother in the RAF. Needless to say, Llewellyn was never loaned another book.

They were invited to the annual Xmas party at the hospital and amongst the guests was the chaplain brother of the Sister on leave from the Navy. He would entertain us on the piano. He asked Glenys to sing and suggested something Welsh. After some words about the music she sang 'Myfanwy' with the first three verses in Welsh and the last verse in English, 'Arabella'. They asked for an encore and she sang 'Y Deryn Pur'. Most of the staff had never heard her sing before and from then on she became a favourite with them. Llewellyn was asked to give a song, but could only remember army songs which they appeared to enjoy, even the spicy words. When he sang 'Calon Lan' Glenys joined in.

The hospital sister had a younger brother who called in to see her and on one occasion shortly after the war finished said he was taking his plane with his crew back to base in Scotland and then would be demobbed. The flight was difficult because of adverse weather conditions and in the fog the plane crashed into the side of a mountain in Yorkshire and all the crew were killed. His brother the naval chaplain went up and conducted the burial service. (The same sheer waste of war spills into the peace with the inevitable and questionable cost of life.)

Glenys and Llewellyn returned to live near his mam and dad a year after the end of the war. Glenys took up part-time nursing and Llewellyn started work with a civil engineering firm. During this time John and Rhys had settled down to civvy life.

When Llewellyn decided to continue his technical education he could not have had a better tutor than Glenys. She was a tremendous help to him and he said on more than one occasion he would not have passed without her help. She would always say, 'Llewellyn, it is easy if you read the question carefully.' Glenys made his promotion to both jobs an easy decision, and with her a part-time district nurse she was able to visit people at their homes instead of seeing them in hospital beds. Usually with each visit there would be a cup of tea waiting for her when she had finished the patient's treatment. Sometimes the patient lived alone. Glenys would make them comfortable in bed and cook a breakfast for them and made sure they ate it before she left. She would say some of the older people who were incapacitated and bed-bound were no better off than some of the servicemen she nursed in hospital. Her round was in a working-class area of Swansea and they openly showed their appreciation of her nursing skills. Llewellyn thought it a most rewarding and satisfying career.

Rhys and John, in spite of taking a long time to settle down at work because of their war service, and even though they never fully recovered their health, would always let Glenys nurse them. Glenys always made sure she first consulted the doctor, who knew her background during the war and was more than pleased of her help. Both were in pain and discomforture, but neither complained, unless it was only to her, which nobody was ever told about. (It was said by Rhys and John that if Glenys had only been brought into the world to spend the years of training to become a nurse for the sole purpose of nursing the two of them, then there could be no greater reward.) Llewelyn saw how they suffered over and over again and Llewellyn thought there were many occasions after both of them had died that her mind was back with them and it was as if only the three of them were in the room and nothing else existed.

Glenys and Llewellyn had a comfortable life together. Their sex life was never a dominant feature, but it was what they both accepted. On those occasions when two people love each other there is never the need for any other company and they were both satisfied that nothing could take that away from them and it was a wish of both of them that when the time came they would want to go together.

Llewellyn suddenly brought himself back from the past as he saw Glenys and Sian by the Cenotaph.

GLENYS SAID TO LLEWELLYN,

'IT IS EASY IF YOU READ THE QUESTION CAREFULLY.'

THE PARADE

When the military band arrived in position facing the Cenotaph the chaplain could be seen with the mayor and his lady, with the political representatives, including the county Lord Lieutenant and his party. There was space near the Cenotaph in spite of such a large number attending but it involved some shuffling around before they settled down and the band started to play the march from *Scipio* by Handel. The Officer commanding the parade could be heard reminding the front of the parade to slow down and mark time. As each contingent moved up and positioned themselves by their marker, so the mark time continued until all the parade were in position.

As the band played softly the Officer commanding could be heard saying:

PARADE HALT AND PARADE TO FACE THE CENOTAPH.
LEFT TURN   PARADE STAND AT EASE.

The chink of medals could then be clearly heard.

STAND EASY.

There was complete silence throughout the parade with the large gathering standing on the pavement. For the first time they appreciated the occasion and the purpose of remembering not only their own relatives who never returned, but others no longer here.

The chaplain asked them to turn to page one of the hymn sheet and as he read out the first line the band started to play, and all around the Cenotaph began to sing.

O valiant heart, who to your glory came,
Through dust of conflict and through battle flame,
Tranquil you lie, your knightly virtue proved,
Your memory hallowed in the land you love.

and finished with the last line of the last verse:

Commits her children to thy gracious hand.

They all sang with equal voice. It was a very moving hymn and the first showing of handkerchiefs could be seen and not only by the older people.

As Llewellyn stood with his fellow comrades the silence after the band finished playing made him tighten his grip on the wreath, and he looked down and saw the name Dad and his thoughts went back to the first memory of him and his eyes started to fill up.

MAM SAID TO LLEWELLYN,

'SHOUT AND TELL DAD HE WILL BE LATE FOR WORK.'

'Shout and tell Dad he will be late for work.'

DAD. Llewellyn's dad always worked nights at the colliery which was about nine miles from their home. It was not that he liked the night shift but because it attracted an additional shift premium of one extra shift pay per week and was a necessity when bringing up a large family. Initially he would travel to work on a lorry with a steel frame on the top, sides, and the back, covered with a tarpaulin sheet secured to the steelwork frame with rope. Inside there were wooden benches for the men to sit on. It was draughty and uncomfortable, but the only means of transport available, other than a cycle. The weekly cost was five shillings (25p).

The proprietor of the lorry in 1936 purchased a second-hand coach to replace the lorry, and the travel arrangements became more formal, but as a private coach it could only pick up private passengers. The coach had three pick up points, and their dad was at the second one. (The cost was not increased.) Pre-war it was not the custom to increase the prices as there was no such thing as annual pay increases/awards. Any rate, employers would not even discuss increases. Their dad used to say any increases since the war were automtically followed by an increase in the cost of living. So who benefits in the end? Another quotation of his was that there is no such thing as competition as the profits of supermarkets were maintained by the items for sale being subject to regular price increases to maintain their 'margins'. If there was competition why do all the supermarkets charge the same prices for the same items?

Their dad would catch the coach for work at 9 pm, and return home at 8 am, but would not go to bed until the after-

32

noon, as he always did some gardening and odd jobs. Hence the reason why he had to be called so often to get him out of bed to go to work. So mam would say to Llewellyn, 'Shout and tell dad he will be late for work.' Their dad was born near Skewen of moderately well-off parents and was the third child. His mam died when she gave birth to him. His dad found it difficult trying to bring up the three children without help, as he worked long hours as an industrial chemist at a local chemical works, so their dad was sent to live with his mam's parents.

In one respect he was fortunate as they both were Welsh speaking and it became his first language and he was able to speak English only after he started school. He was a good learner and was also taught to play the piano and completed all grades up to and including diploma.

His grandparents were religious and he went to chapel with them from a young age and that was part of the early formation of his life. He had a good singing voice and played the piano at chapel events and later played the chapel organ when the regular organist was absent. His grandparents idolised him. When he left school with a good education he obtained employment at one of the local pits, as there was little choice of any other work. Life underground was not only hard, but conditions were dreadful, with water dripping from the roof, and foul smelling air. The lighting was by approved paraffin safety lamps made by Messrs E Thomas and Williams of Aberdare and other suppliers.

It was no life for a young man with such good talent and a flair for music. Their dad met their mam at a combined Sunday school meeting which she attended with her sisters. She was shy and it was a long time before they even spoke to each other. Her being church and their dad being chapel made it difficult. She was never able to meet him without one of her sisters being present. Mainly they had to be satisfied with only a smile. However, where young people are concerned, an attraction between them they will find a reason and the time to see each other, and they eventually started seeing each other when she started to work in a shop in the village, but never until 9 pm when the shop closed.

Their dad would wait for her and walk home to her house which was about two miles away. Outside the house they would talk for a few minutes and as soon as she heard her mam calling she would go in without even a hint of a kiss. Once her mam knew she was seeing someone regularly she suggested her daughter invite him home for Sunday tea. This became a feature of their courtship. He only met her dad once as most of the time he was on overtime at the colliery where he worked in the stables underground looking after the horses.

Sometimes his grandparents would invite her to tea on a Sunday. By this time most of the relatives knew they were going together, or seeing each other, as people would say. There was little opportunity to indulge in anything other than holding hands, with a tight-lipped kiss. They both appeared to be content just to walk together and talk incessantly to each other, about nothing in particular, and for no reason start giggling.

Early in 1916 their dad was informed he was being called up for active service in the Hampshire Regiment, and proceeded to Winchester for training. After completing his infantry training he was given seven days' embarkation leave before going to France. When the train arrived at Neath railway station she was waiting for him and told him she had been given the afternoon off and also two days before the end of his leave.

They made a special effort to spend as much time together as possible. It would be late nights. Each day they went somewhere different on the few days holiday she had. Swansea to a show and a day at Mumbles. Usually they would have a meal before he returned her home. Halfway through his leave he proposed to her and she accepted. Both families were delighted with the news. They went into Neath and bought the engagement ring and spent the remainder of the day showing it off to relatives and friends.

In the evening of the last full day of his leave they went for a walk along the canal bank. On the way back to her home there appeared to be an underlying excitement between them and they held each other's hands more tightly. They both without telling the other seemed to have decided whatever happened before the night was over would happen irrespective of the consequences.

When he called the next morning he received an odd look from her mam. He felt his face going red and looked away from her.

34

After they said their goodbyes, both full of love for the other, he asked her to marry him on his next leave, and almost before she could answer him the train was there and he was on his way. They wrote regularly over the next six months. She kept all his letters in a neat bundle. (They are still in her possession.)

Both families were helping with the wedding arrangements in anticipation of his next leave. Shortly before he was due home his grandparents received notification he was reported missing, believed killed. They took the telegram over to show her, but she could not stop crying and she wished she had told him she was having his child. About three months later a letter arrived to say he was in a prisoner of war camp in Germany.

He arrived home from Germany in January 1919. He looked ill and could not settle down. He had difficulty sleeping and developed a hacking cough which never left him all his life. With both families making the wedding arrangements he started to improve. They were married in February 1919 and moved to 'rooms' in Skewen. They had started married life with a ready-made family, but other children were soon on the way. By 1940 they had a family of six boys and two girls.

Their dad did not have an easy life because he was dogged with ill health. He never complained and would go to work even if he had to drag himself. He kept a good garden and they were never short of vegetables. They had a chicken run with a good supply of eggs and chicken dinners were a regular Sunday meal. All the children were born at home, and the day after a baby was born their mam had to leave the bed and start her housework. The midwife could call after the birth to provide any nursing or treatment. There were no such luxuries as home help.

Their dad prior to being a haulier worked on the coal face. It required him to fill many trams of coal per shift. Each full tram would be marked on the side of the tram in chalk with his lamp number. When the full tram eventually reached the surface it would be weighed for coal content less small coal and small lumps on the weighbridge. The nett coal weight would be creditted to his lamp number. He received 2/6 pence per ton (13p). He would be paid for all the timber erected on the face, to compensate the space made when the coal was removed. Each yard the face moved forward sleepers and rails were laid. If he had a helper he would be responsible for his wages. His shovels, sledge, pick, chisels and drilling equipment would have to be bought. Explosives would be provided. When he changed from being a miner to a haulier through ill-health his wages were reduced to approx two thirds of the miners' wage.

During the 1926 miners' strike, with no money coming in, their dad would go to the slag tip with a pick and shovel and dig for small lumps of coal. It would take about four hours to fill one sack. He would convey it home on an old pram. Coal was the only form of heating and cooking. Meat was never on the menu, unless he caught a rabbit and all the chickens had already been killed. Their dad never picked more small coal than he needed. On occasions a policeman would watch from a hiding place and just as their dad and the other men started to carry it away he would reveal his presence and chase them. They would have to drop the full sack. If caught there would be a fine, or a prison sentence.

He became the deputy organist at the chapel he attended, and received a small remuneration when called on to deputise – 7/6 (37p). The chapel and playing the organ gave him a spiritual uplift to compensate for the hard and little rewarding colliery work. Also he would take the children with him for the morning and evening service. Their mam could then prepare the meals without interruptions. In those days chapels were always full on Sundays. On the Remembrance Sunday morning service their dad would make sure the children who were old enough to attend were there. Their highlight was the playing of the Last Post by one of the local bandsmen.

The children made regular visits to see their grandfather and step-grandmother with their dad, but were never able to remember what he looked like. It seemed he was always preoccupied when they were there and he could not think of their first names however many times they told him. Their dad's health slowly deteriorated over the years and the poor working conditions underground did little to help. An accident at the colliery triggered off further problems. He was unable to work and it was thought he would die, but recovered his health slowly. Their mam took in washing clothes, cleaned other people's houses and even papered. She was the only source of money coming into the house. The only day she had for herself was Sunday, and even then she had to clean the house through and prepare Sunday meals.

Then their dad was well enough to return to work. (He said it was due to his unshakable faith in God who helped him during his illness.) It was not easy for him to cope with the job but as his confidence returned and he was again bringing in a wage he settled down to working the night shift. The colliery closed down soon after the start of the Second World War, and their dad was drafted to a metal producing works some miles away. He was allocated a house which was only two years old. It was like paradise after the old house in Skewen. A semi-detached property with three bedrooms, two living rooms, a modern kitchen and a large bathroom and toilet. Plus a large garden and a brick air-raid shelter. He had a responsible job in the fabrication department and on war work. Again a lot of overtime, which was the last thing he wanted if his health was to improve.

Their mam started a part-time job in the post room where their dad worked. With her four eldest sons in the armed forces she wanted something to do without having to think of them. She would send them money whenever possible. Sian and Andrew were still at school. They both shared the housework and shopping, but the bulk of it fell on Sian. It must not be forgotten she also looked after Avril. Sian was a bright person and liked to keep in the background unless it was to help her older brothers, when she would be first off the mark.

Living near the docks were troops, and their vehicles would be parked for periods up to a week before being shipped overseas gave their mam the chance to provide them with home cooking. Whenever she made cakes and tarts extra would be made and given to the troops. They would reciprocate with some tins of corned beef. Their mam and dad would say they only did what they hoped other people would do for their sons.

When their mam and dad were informed by telegram Gareth was dead (Killed in Action) it was unbearable, and for the first time they looked old and vulnerable. Their dad was more upset than he showed as Gareth was his favourite, not that it was noticeable in front of the other sons. It took a long time before he got over the loss, and one had to be careful not to mention Gareth's name in his company.

Glenys and Llewellyn were married on his return from overseas. This seemed to brighten him up and he came down for the wedding with Sian and Andrew.

Their dad said the war would not last long once the invasion of Normandy was under way. VE Day followed quickly. He now looked forward to his sons coming home. This soon arrived and demobbed and after a while it seemed as though they had never been away. Their dad's health improved and the family looked forward to Sunday lunch and tea at home, the two meals they always remembered when overseas. When the table was cleared after tea one of them said what about going out for a drink. It was one of the few occasions they went out on a Sunday night. It was partly to do with not being able to settle down properly and as if they had lost something from when they left home in 1939. It was not easy for the family as they all tried to appear normal, but it certainly was not easy.

Their dad noticed how ill John and Rhys were, and saw no improvement as the months went by. Neither had any colour and had bent shoulders. They appeared to have jumped from young men to old men and in a short space of only six years.

The weddings and the coming of children did a lot to bring hope for the future. John left for Australia. His dad missed him more than he said, as he would always remember he was two years old before he saw him. The piano was his therapy and he would spend hours in the front room playing for himself. Sometimes their mam would go in and they would both harmonise the songs they knew from many years ago. They were as close during those times as when they first married. It was this love which remained the sheet-anchor of the family.

The Edwards' family made the most of the period immediately after the war in spite of the setbacks and loss of loved ones and the others dogged with ill-health. At the wedding of Avril their dad caught a cold and it took a long time before he could shake it off and he never really got over it.

Their holidays were usually spent with Glenys and

Llewellyn, and on their last holiday with them he did not seem to enjoy it as he usually did, and could not settle down, or take any interest in his meals. Llewellyn tried to make their stay enjoyable, with trips to where their dad spent holidays as a child. In the middle of the second week he said he would like to go home. On the last evening Llewellyn and his dad went out for a drink, and just before they finished their drinks he asked Llewellyn to promise to look after his mam if anything happened to him. Thinking back over the conversation it was as if he knew he did not have long to live. His dad knew Llewellyn did not have to answer him, but for peace of mind he said yes.

Not long after they returned home he was rushed into hospital. Llewellyn went to see him, and was reminded of the promise he made. He died a few weeks later and probably without any regrets as it would be an end to the suffering he had endured since his return from the First world war.

MAM SAID TO LLEWELLYN,

'SHOUT AND TELL DAD HE WILL BE LATE FOR WORK.'

THE PARADE

The Officer commanding the parade read out the lesson. He had removed his bowler hat and as he looked around at the large gathering put on his glasses before he started and removed his notes from inside of his bowler hat. During the reading of the lesson it could be seen he was having to gather his thoughts and hesitated before continuing with the reading of the lesson. He knew, like all ex-service personnel, the occasion made it difficult to keep his thoughts under control. He cleared his throat, and touched his face with an handkerchief, and it was noticeable the strain as he looked at them all, and could see their medals showing a mass of colour.

Then in a clear voice he started to read:

> 'Seeing the crowds, Jesus went up on the mountain and when he sat down his disciples came to him, and he opened his mouth and taught them to say, Blessed are the poor in spirit for theirs is the Kingdom of Heaven'.

The Officer commanding concluded the lesson with:

> 'Rejoice and be glad for your reward is great in heaven, for so men persecuted the prophets who were before you'.

He replaced his notes inside his hat and removed his glasses. Then it was on with the bowler.

Llewellyn holding on to his wreath thought how difficult it had been for the Edwards' family, not only during the war but before the war.

As Llewellyn collected his thoughts so he remembered his mam.

MAM SAID TO LLEWELLYN,

'ASK DAD TO MAKE THE MINT SAUCE.'

40

MAM SAID TO LLEWELLYN,

'ASK DAD TO MAKE THE MINT SAUCE.'

MAM came from a large family of four girls and two boys. Her father worked in a colliery a few miles outside the village. When he first started there he would walk to and from the colliery every day, until he could afford a second-hand cycle. (There was no public transport from Jersey Marine then.) The colliery he worked in was owned by Bevans and Evans.

The family had a hard time making ends meet and lived on a small farm, or it could even be called a smallholding, of about thirty acres of land on the side of the mountain. The only means of transport was a horse and cart and the horse would double-up pulling a plough, and other farming implements. They normally used the land for grazing the livestock, and market gardening. The livestock consisted of cows, pigs, chickens, ducks and some turkey at Xmas. They would sell most of the produce to supplement their meagre income, but the family always had a staple diet. Their dad would slaughter pigs regularly and they would be sold in the village.

All the children had their own jobs to do before going to school and again when they returned home from school. Feeding chickens and ducks was a favourite of the girls, and collecting the eggs. Chickens had their own places to lay so it was not an easy task finding the eggs. It's what is now known as free-range. The eggs were usually sold from a large wicker basket and even then the customers would from choice pick the brown eggs.

There was a small duck pond. In the summer it would dry up and in the winter it would overflow and freeze over. The children under the watchful eyes of the older ones would spend hours sliding on the ice.

Their job tasks were changed about. They never liked milking, but liked to help with butter and cheese making. When the cow needed servicing the older boys would take the cow over to another farm for the bull. On one occasion the young bull was small and when he put his front legs on the back of the cow and the farmer held the cow's tail away, so the bull's rear legs slipped underneath the cow on its back. It took a lot of time and patience before the cow was eventually serviced. When a calf was born and it was a bull calf every one was delighted. The milk yield of the cow after birth was very high, thick and a deep yellow. It would only be used to feed the calf, and the surplus would be put down the drain. After about six milkings it could then be used for human consumption. Each milking would produce about six gallons of milk. Most farmers would wean the calf by hand directly from a pail.

The bull calf would either be taken to market to be sold shortly after birth or kept for about up to two years old then sold as beef. When possible their dad would take the children with him and they would spend their time looking around the shops or the stalls in the market. It would always be a long process deciding what to buy with their pocket money and they would share the cost of a present for their mam and dad.

If he had a good price for the animal, he would call in for a few drinks. He always liked the beer at The Market Vaults. The children would wait outside, but he would take them out a soft drink. When they were ready to leave the boys would fetch the horse and cart, the journey home would be slow as their dad would start singing and the girls would have to join in. Having their tea after the trip to Neath would be noisy when they showed their mam what they bought. The sweets bought were not for sharing and were never hurriedly eaten but only a few taken to school, and would last them a long time.

The small farm only made a small profit, but without it and only a small wage at the colliery they would not have managed, and it is worth remembering there was no DHSS to fall back on. Their mam would say there was something special about living on a farm which could not compensate them as each day was always different, and it would only need one to look out of the window any morning to know this was true as there were never two days alike. When it was fine and clear one could see out over the Swansea Bay at the ships lying at anchor. To breathe the fresh air gave a lift to keep one going all day.

One of the favourite jobs was to take the horse to the blacksmith for shoeing. The oldest boy would lead the horse and one of the girls would sit on the back. There was always an argument which girl should go, but they were always able to settle it amongst themselves. The least liked job was the regular trip by all the family to collect firewood down on the beach which was nearly two miles away. The boys would hitch up the horse to the cart and fit a long post to each corner of the cart and secure with rope. The journey down was easy with an empty cart. At the beach they would all help to collect wood brought in by the tide. When they stopped for a 'spell' their mam handed round sandwiches and homemade lemonade.

Once the cart was full the load was secured with rope and the journey back to the farm was slow and required the strength of all the family to push and pull the cart as it was too heavy for the horse on its own. By the time they reached the top they would all be covered in perspiration even in the middle of the winter. A full load of wood usually lasted about two months and then back to the beach. In the summer it was more pleasant as they could have a swim and a proper picnic.

Sometimes they were fortunate to find a fallen tree and it would quickly be sawn up. It should be remembered they did not have electricity or gas for heating and cooking. Their dad did receive an allocation of coal four times per year, but as there was not a proper road up to the farm the coal would be off-loaded about 400 yards away and collected by horse and cart.

Schooling was not easy as there was a walk of two miles each way. They enjoyed learning and as a family made the most of the opportunity. The oldest girl eventually became a school teacher in Swansea. Homework was a must and they did receive some help from their mam, but within a short time had passed her standard.

Sunday school was never missed. They walked there in the afternoon, and their dad would fetch them with the horse and cart. They were well-versed in the scriptures and always able to obtain top marks for answering scripture questions.

The children all helped when the pigs were slaughtered, and always carried out on a Thursday afternoon after school. Their dad would do the killing by putting a sharp knife into the throat of the pig and severing the main artery to let it bleed to death. The children would scrub the pig in very hot water to remove the bristles. It certainly was hard work. Their dad would lift the carcass on to a hook, cut from the top of throat to the tail and remove the offal and entrails. These would be cleaned in very hot water to make chitterlings. Afterwards it would be cut into small joints. All the meat was ordered in advance and the children would take the orders to the customers. There would not be much left for the family, unless two pigs were slaughtered. However, they always had the belly pork which all the family liked. The offal from the pig (liver-lights-meat pieces) would be minced and seasoned with onions and herbs. The minced meat would be put into deep sided trays and scored into small squares, or faggots, and after an apron of suet covered the faggots they were cooked in the oven. Dried peas would soak overnight and be boiled the next morning. Beef bones were boiled slowly in a large pan to render them down. The wonderful aroma from the pan made the family hungry. The faggots and peas were now ready, and would be taken to houses of those who put in an order. Others would collect themselves. The orders would be made up in large basins or jugs with the faggots and gravy stock in the one and the peas in the other. It was certainly a busy morning for all of them. Once all the orders were dealt with the family would sit down to their meal. Each would have a big soup plate of faggots and peas swimming in gravy stock. It was only necessary to add pepper and vinegar. There would always be a plate of freshly baked bread. By the time the meal was finished, they were all too full to move and would then say as a chorus, 'a meal fit for a king'.

They would argue amongst themselves which part of the meal was best and some said the faggots, others the peas or gravy stock, and finally the new bread. One would even say the pepper and vinegar. They never resolved which part of the meal they liked individually. The last part of the pig to be used was the head which would finish up as brawn, and one of their favourites for tea. The bladder was cleaned and made into a football.

When a number of pigs were slaughtered and cut up their dad would salt down sides of the pig into bacon which would be hung in a cool pantry until cured. To have home cured bacon and eggs for breakfast is the luxury only those who lived on a farm can fully appreciate and the wonderful smell of the bacon being fried could not be bought.

Bath night was on a Saturday. The girls in the living room and the boys in the back kitchen using galvanised baths. It meant keeping a large fire going to heat the water. When they all finished they would sit in front of the warm fire with a mug of cocoa and then off to bed. Whilst wood and coal were the main source of heating they did have a portable paraffin heater, but it was very smoky. Lighting downstairs was a ritual insomuch as the 'oil lamps' were polished each day and the glass protecting the paraffin flame would have to be cleaned to remove soot. The two lamps were sufficient to light their large living room. Upstairs they would have candles.

There were no radios in those days and they could not afford a daily paper, but did buy *The News of the World* each Sunday. The children were not allowed to read it, but their mam knew they all read it. It was a good source of current affairs to equip them later in life. On Monday mornings the Sunday paper was cut into small squares with cord threaded through and would be taken to the stone built WC about twenty yards from the house and hung on a nail. (Anything they missed in the Sunday paper could be read there.) Inside the WC was a large bucket, and over it was a wooden seat of planks secured to the sides of the wall with a hole over the bucket. It was their dad's job to empty the bucket when full. In the winter the family were most reluctant to use the WC after dark. If absolutely necessary, their mam would have to go out with them and stand guard outside the WC until they finished.

By today's standards life seemed terribly hard, but they all had a good grounding to start their own lives. Their ability to keep house and appreciate the value of money was ingrained into them. Through watching their mam cooking came naturally to them.

The birds and bees explanation was not necessary as the cycle of animal life on the farm which they saw happening every day gave them an insight to some of the answers to questions about their own bodies. They loved nothing better than watching the birth of calves and piglets, and helping with their first start in life.

There were few jobs for girls when they left school other

than to be in service or shop work. There was some office work, but they would more likely go to relatives than outsiders, unless they had more than the acceptable level of educational abilities. The girls were strong and had few illnesses and grew into lovely young women. Their unblemished skin owed a lot to wholesome food and in spite of there being no restrictions on how much they could eat they never put on an ounce of excess weight. Their exercise consisted of walking to school and back in the evening, and the contribution they all made to the farm work expected of them. They usually met their 'Futures' at church and chapel, married young and had lots of children.

Their mam and dad became engaged before he left for France and she said it was the happiest day of her life and the week they had together when he was on embarkation leave was marvellous beyond her wildest dreams. For all that she could be practical and down-to-earth which could be expected of someone brought up on a farm and therefore had made her mind up that if there was to be more than kissing she would not stop herself being an active partner. But the thought would bring a blush to her cheek when thinking about it. When the opportunity came on the last full day of his leave she knew when they stopped near her home and sat against the hedge that she had no control over the events when they took over and could think of nothing else other than being a participating partner in the love making.

Two months after he went to France she knew she was having a baby. When she told her mam she expected some words, but to her surprise she could not be more pleased. He wrote back from the 'Front Line' and told her to make the arrangements to get married on his next leave. But this was not to be so as he was captured by the Germans.

When they settled down to married life after the First World War they had a hard life together, with his illness taking precedence over their early married life, which meant she had to go out to work to bring in money. The work was not easy and mainly washing other people's clothes, cleaning work, and even papering rooms. In fact anything they wanted doing. It was a wonder how they managed, and coupled with bringing up children it meant hard times until the start of the Second World War.

46

The mobilisation of her four oldest sons into the Armed Forces left a big gap in the family. This made her more protective towards the other children. Whenever war news came on the radio their mam was almost afraid to listen to it, or concentrate on what she was doing. She always had a premonition about the eventual fate of Rhys, but it was Gareth who was killed, and the least expected. She took his death hard and would say of Gareth the most gentle of her sons he deserved better than to die hundreds of miles from her. Their dad would remind her that all her sons were vulnerable, and not just the one. To a mother, and in spite of favourites, her suffering was for all of them. The war could not be over soon enough for her, and in the end she was thankful for the return of the rest of them.

On the first opportunity after the end of the war they had one of the Sunday lunches and teas which were special before the war, with as many of the family as possible attending. She said, as she did on many occasions before the war, would Llewellyn ask his dad to make the mint sauce'?

All her sons were loved by their mam, but the favourite, even though she tried to hide it, was Rhys, and the look on her face when he walked into the house or someone mentioned his name something to be wondered at. It was as if they were both walking on a single track, and no one could overtake or separate them. The pain Rhys suffered up to the end, and which was shared by his mam, could only be described as a fine thread between them which could with the smallest tug break. Her decline in health started from then and after the death of her third son it was realised the high price her family had to pay. Shortly afterwards she sold the house and went to live with her daughter Sian.

MAM SAID TO LLEWELLYN,

'ASK DAD TO MAKE THE MINT SAUCE.'

THE PARADE

As Llewellyn collected his thoughts Phillip asked if there was anything the matter and he turned and shook his head.

Llewellyn could hear the chaplain telling them to turn to page three of the hymn sheet and read out the first line. As he finished the band started to play, and the congregation began to sing:

> Guide me, O thou great Redeemer,
> Pilgrim through this barren land.
> I am weak, but thou art mighty,
> Hold me with thy powerful hand.
> Bread of Heaven,
> Feed me now and evermore.

And after the last line of the last verse was finished,

> I will ever give to thee,

there was a change in the mood of those present as the chaplain began telling them of his war service when he was a young soldier during the Italian Campaign. He was not trying to put forward his own importance, but providing a gentle reminder of the conditions on active service. The chaplain continued with his thoughts of his war service, and some of the ex-servicemen were getting restless, but to their relief he stopped.

Ex-service people normally do not discuss their war service and consider the annual attendance on Remembrance Sunday and wearing their medals a sufficient reminder.

Llewellyn felt the wreath in his hand, and thought back.

ANDREW WOULD SAY TO LLEWELLYN,

*'MAM ALWAYS LOOKS THROUGH THE
FRONT WINDOW FOR ME.'*

48

ANDREW WOULD SAY TO LLEWELLYN,

'Mam always looks through the front window for me.'

ANDREW was the youngest son in the family and without any doubt was the most loved because of his kind ways and always calling in to see his mam and dad. Andrew was looked upon as the baby of the family, especially by his mam who had a special place in her heart for him. He was born in the thirties, and following the long illness of his dad as there was just a glimpse of improvement. However, with John and Llewellyn bringing in a wage each the family were able to manage. As a baby Andrew was the pride and joy of the family and neighbours. When taken out in his pram comments would be made about the ready smile on his face. He hardly ever cried and was very contented. As he grew up he became a loyal part of the family. Even though he was not particularly shy he would wait outside the house until his older brothers came home from work but would not go in the house, but wait until they went out and walk with them to the end of the road.

When Glenys came over from the hospital on her afternoon off Andrew would wait until he saw her coming up the road and when near enough would walk in front of her. When she caught him up she would hold his hand and they would walk together. He would only talk in answer to a question put to him, otherwise said little else. Andrew only half looked at her, but always had his wonderful smile for her and she remembers it to this day. When they were sitting at the table he always strove to sit next to her. On her return to hospital he would walk her to the end of the road, and with a quick 'So-long', was gone.

When the family moved to where their dad was working Andrew took some time to settle down but once he found his way around started to make new friends and the new neighbours quickly took to him. He did not see Glenys so often, but still never lost the habit of waiting near the house until she appeared and walking to the house with her. His mam and dad were still over-protective towards him. His older brothers would think it because he had been ill and unable to do his National Service. Any rate the seven years' difference between him and the next oldest brother was too big a gap to maintain continuity with them.

Andrew was a natural diver and swimmer, and would if possible have spent all his time in the swimming pool. Diving was his first love and if he had been coached he would have represented his county. Even his breaststroke technique was the subject of comment from others.

On leaving school he obtained employment with a furniture manufacturer who specialised in three-piece suites, and dining room furniture. He settled down to the job quickly and trained to assemble the suites as the first part of his training programme. He was next transferred to the machine shop and given training to operate specialist wood turning machines used for forming the legs of chairs. Within a few years he had been trained to involve himself with all the manufacturing processes. The firm were licensed to produce utility furniture to standards laid down by the government.

During his initial training he attended the local technical school for two years, and obtained his City and Guild certificate in cabinetmaking. With the additional training he began to have more confidence in his ability to work with others. He was tall and good-looking and naturally was interested in the opposite sex. The girls started to call at his home and ask for him. His mam and dad were more than pleased and even slightly amused by the interest shown in him by the fairer sex. When the war ended in 1945 he still continued with night school to improve himself, and to counteract the disappointment in not being able to do National Service. He included in his curriculum a course on supervision. By this time he was beginning to attract the attention of management. He was now leading a full life and therefore always broke before the end of the week, and it was his mam who would lend him money to tide him over until the end of the week, but on the pay of an improver/apprentice there was little hope of him being able to pay her back. Andrew was good with his hands and did all the repairs to the house, including the decorating and gardening. It was his way of paying his mam and dad back for the money he had from them every week.

The difference in age between Owen and Andrew was only three years and Owen had been a good influence on him, and apart from the time Owen was in the Royal Air Force they have always been more than brothers. Andrew was a good learner, with the ability to retain information, but how he was able to cope with night school, the girls, his job and never be late for work amazed everyone. When the three remaining sons returned home from war service it tended to reduce Andrew from being oldest to youngest overnight. It was a difficult adjustment to make and it was understandable he wanted to kick over the traces, but eventually his natural ability to be liked, and a few words from his brothers, soon brought things back to normal.

It was a worrying time for their mam and dad with Andrew being somewhat difficult when his brothers came home, and the last thing they wanted was a family problem, but it was as well for Andrew to know his brothers were home for good. When Owen returned from National Service and had been married on his last leave they were able to share some of their previous ways. Andrew did start to make new friends, and not look to his older brothers for anything other than brotherly companionship. It was also difficult for him at his workplace, as further ajustments were necessary with the return of the ex-service personnel to jobs they held before they were called up.

With the demand for furniture, and a large backlog to catch up on it meant overtime and he was able to forget his troubles. Andrew, because of his technical training and a sound pro-duct knowledge, was made a junior foreman. His fellow workmates resented the promotion he was given. Andrew was not able to appreciate or understand the men he was respons-ible for had themselves in the war held a rank, and were res-ponsible for the men under them, and for someone so young to be put in charge of them took a lot of understanding. To avoid bad feeling he offered to stand down from the foreman's job. He decided to have a chat with Rhys about the difficult situation that was developing. Rhys suggested to him to wait a few weeks before acting on any decision as it was likely the problem would die a natural death, and Rhys reminded him he was given the promotion because management considered him the best qualified person for the position. Andrew had a lot to learn about people, but was beginning to find out quickly, and to his credit he never forgot what Rhys said to him.

Andrew decided to have a talk with the Managing Director as well who agreed with him it would be better to leave the subject in abeyance, or until someone else brought it up. He did go to great lengths to see their point of view and fully appreciated the frankness of all concerned. He had target figures to meet and if they were not achieved he would be accountable. He soon realised why he was given the job to improve production figures. It was necessary to introduce some overtime to reduce the backlog.

The introduction of new furniture design and installation of specialist machinery and equipment coupled with new materials was a challenge, but showed he was capable of introducing and explaining the techniques required to operate the new machinery, and use the materials on the shopfloor. The work force soon realised why Andrew had been given the promotion. With the ability physically to demonstrate the new procedures Andrew would not have to wait too long before he would be considered for further promotion.

To cope with the increase in demand for their products there was a further increase in female labour on the shopfloor. Andrew being popular with girls was regularly dating them and it seemed as though there was a different one every time. This was proving to be an embarrassment as foremen were expected to ensure their private life to be separate from work. In the end Andrew received a private word from management. It was also the occasion of him being told a new management position was being created to coincide with the heavy workload and the need to expand. He suggested to Andrew he applied. Shortly afterwards the position was advertised on the works' noticeboard. Andrew put in his application and with others was interviewed by the managing director. A week later he was offered the position and accepted. To himself he thought he may have taken on too much as he was still attending night school twice a week.

The obvious solution for Andrew as far as the girls were concerned came in the form of a young and attractive secretary to the managing director, and with his new promotion would have regular contact with her as he was now directly responsible as production manager to him. She knew about his shopfloor reputation with the girls and she made her mind up to have nothing to do with him. However, his regular meetings with the managing director made it difficult as she could not avoid talking to him on works' matters and Andrew, being persistent, kept asking her to go out with him, but she had already decided the answer would always be no.

As time went on everybody from the managing director to the shopfloor labourers knew of the unspoken fight going on between Megan and Andrew, but both were oblivious to this, especially Megan in her determination to have nothing to do with him. Andrew still had the feeling beneath it all she was interested in him and by using all the tricks in the book he had a chance, but to outsiders it did not look as if either would win. (This was one of the occasions when he regretted his activities with other girls.) To Megan there was the element of excitement of the unknown which made him attractive to others.

Even though there were no bets as to who would win, that is if winning was the only object both were aiming for, it was getting to the stage when both were neglecting their work. The managing director decided to involve himself otherwise there would be no end to the confrontation as with each refusal by Megan when asked for a date resulted in him asking one of the shopfloor girls to go out with him and he made sure she found out. It all seemed as though he was digging a hole deeper and deeper. The managing director arranged for them both to work together preparing a projected set of production figures for calculating labour requirements and to be ready by the following morning. Andrew would prepare the report and Megan type it. When completed he asked both separately to have dinner with him as a just reward for staying on. When they arrived at the managing director's office and as he was waiting for them they had no alternative but to accept.

During the dinner with only the managing director contributing to the conversation it seemed as though it would never end and all they made were disinterested replies to anything he said. Slowly there was a slight thawing in the atmosphere between them. After the dinner and not before time as far as the managing director was concerned he offered them both a lift home and again they found it difficult to refuse. The MD drove to his home and as he stopped said to Andrew, 'You take the car and drop Megan off and pick me up in the morning.' Megan looked at the MD, and thought this dinner is not a reward for completing the report but a pre-arranged assignation. She was thankful and reasonably sure Andrew knew nothing about it.

The drive to her home was without incident and as she got out of the car he put his hand upon hers partly to stop her leaving, and asked her if he could see her the following evening, and with her head down she gave the briefest of nods, said goodnight and was gone. He sat in the car for a long time thinking of the events of the evening and said to himself, 'Progress at last' but kept his fingers crossed just in case anything went wrong.

From the evening of the dinner it was as if neither knew anyone else, or had time for others. At the weekly production meeting which Andrew attended Megan made sure the first cup of tea was given to him and in spite of the sugar shortage he would have his usual three spoonfuls plus first refusal of the biscuits. The MD was more than pleased with his timely intervention as it was proving to be the correct action.

The courtship was longish and they lived for each other, but she was strict that they should not see each other more than twice per week away from the works. This was something Megan insisted on. Both families wondered whether it was to test him, but for all that it did work without any difficulties. All this time Megan did not make life easy for him and the least sign of being taken for granted would result in either her walking away and saying 'Is this how you treat your other girlfriends'? Megan was determined from the beginning their courtship would not be a one-sided affair to suit Andrew only and that he had to learn to respect her and the way she behaved towards him, and slowly their love for each other developed and grew into something better than she expected.

Andrew tried to take their love-making a stage further than the kissing. She would stop him and, looking straight into his face, say it was entirely up to him if he wanted sex now, or wait until they were married. Given the choice and knowing she would not go back on her word, Andrew did not know how to deal with the situation and would back away. Megan was no fool and she now felt more sure of Andrew's feelings towards her and knew he would not in the future proceed further than some very frantic kissing.

When they decided to get married they looked around for a suitable house. Both saved hard during their courtship and were able to put a deposit down, with sufficient money to decorate and buy some furniture. Most of the time up to the marriage was spent preparing the house so they would be able to move in straight away after the wedding.

They had a wonderful day for the wedding and both families with friends attending. Megan kept her job Andrew having to work longer hours, and she was on shorter hours than him enabling her to prepare the evening meal when he came home. Initially they wanted to be on their own and concentrate on the house and garden, but it was over two years before they were satisfied with the results. They made sure they went out once during the week to the pictures, a meal and a few drinks. Saturday night would be spent with the family or friends at the local pub. (It should be remembered there was no television in the early years after the war.)

Megan knew about Andrew when it came to other women, even though it was not a hard-won reputation as dating other women came easy to him. Though he tried hard to put down the past it was not always within his control, and he found it difficult when explaining to Megan he was trying to put the past behind him and that it would take some time. Megan partly understood and wondered if she was too firm with him and still not trusting him. Over the years of their marriage both had rows, some extremely fierce, and it brought out the so-called flaw in his character about other women. Megan could be cold towards him and this tended to frustrate him all the more and revive his interest in the other women.

Not knowing all the answers, or even what the question was, Andrew decided to talk to Rhys. They went for a drink and Rhys listened to Andrew. All Rhys could say was the first thing he should do was to definitely stop seeing other women. He eventually made Andrew promise this. Rhys looked at him

55

and said, 'You'd better make sure you keep your promise', and even though Andrew was taller and more heavily built than Rhys he did for a few seconds feel afraid, and remembered Rhys had fought with the Ghurkas in the Far East. This was coupled with the unexplainable fear Rhys would not fight fair against him if he found out he did not keep his promise. Rhys would say the Japanese never gave anyone a second chance, and also the British army had taught him how to kill but not how not to kill.

Andrew realised he was fast losing Megan's trust and also risking the wrath of Rhys, and full well knowing the bond between him and Megan borne out by her instinct that Rhys possessed a knowledge or insight not based on worldly logic, but something defined as mystery beyond human intelligence, and not unlike a military order which is never the subject for discussion. The talk with Rhys appeared to defuse the problem between them, with Andrew becoming more of a man in the true sense of the word and not because he holds down a responsible job.

Andrew had from the time he was married called in to see his mam on his way home from work. It would only be for a few minutes but he always felt the better for it. She would look out of the window until she saw him, and by the time he came through the back door she had a cup of tea and a slice of cake ready for him. Seeing him also reminded her of when he was a boy with a very special smile. The bond between him and his mam was not a side many people knew about. Andrew and Megan took it upon themselves to do the heavy work in the garden, cut the lawn and do all the planting. They would regularly decorate the inside and outside of the house. They considered it their contribution to the well-being of their mam and dad.

After Avril and Ivor married and moved away Andrew was more then ever determined to make sure they were all right, and started to call on a Sunday morning with her Sunday newspaper.

Andrew could not understand why they were having problems with their marriage. He should have known if he remembered the difficulties he had getting the first date with her. Probably if he had given enough thought to it he would have realised a larger part of the blame was his, but being stubborn it was not easy to admit he could be in the wrong. He realised they were getting into a rut, and not enjoying their sex life as they should. Andrew started to return to his old habit of seeing the shopfloor girls after work, and knowing it was wrong could not find an alternative solution. It was some months before he had reason to doubt his own preconceived views on sex and realised he had a gem of a partner in Megan when she decided to take control of their love-making, discreetly, so as not to show Andrew how selfish and one-sided his sexual behaviour was. Andrew and Megan never looked back after the episode when she decided to change things, and their love for each other changed. Andrew started to bring her home a present in the form of a gift or a bunch of flowers.

Andrew continued to make inroads into his position at work, and within another four years was offered promotion to general manager on the retirement of his predecessor. At work the range of products were contained, and individual styles simplified to increase the production runs. They also introduced self-assembly kitchen packs.

ANDREW WOULD SAY TO LLEWELLYN,

*'Mam always looks through the
front window for me.'*

THE PARADE

When the chaplain said to turn to page three of the hymn sheet so he started to read the first line.

> The Lord's my Shepherd, I'll not want,

those present with the shuffling of feet and the clearing of throats heard the band start to play, and opening their hymn sheets started to sing.

> The Lord's my Shepherd, I'll not want,
> He makes me down to lie
> In pastures green; He leadeth me
> The quiet waters by.

It would seem as the hymn was being sung the poignancy of the occasion was most noticeable, and the more visible signs of some of them being upset.

When the last line was sung,

> My dwelling place shall be,

a hush came over the gathering and for some seconds not a sound could be heard. Even though it was cold with sufficient wind to make the flags flutter it did not make any difference to the people gathered around the Cenotaph.

Looking at those at the service it was refreshing to note the number of younger people at the service and their interest in the formality of the occasion and Llewellyn's thoughts went back to the time when the name Megan was first mentioned. He wondered what sort of person she was and when she came to Sunday tea it was noticeable how well she got on with Andrew's mam and dad. Llewellyn felt the wreath in his hand and held it all the more tightly as he said to himself, 'Megan, what have you let yourself in for?'

MEGAN SAID TO LLEWELLYN,

'Why did it have to be Rhys who died?'

58

MEGAN SAID TO LLEWELLYN,

'Why did it have to be Rhys who died?'

MEGAN came on the scene not by choice, but through her association with Andrew at their workplace. She had no intention of being involved as the gossip in the factory was rife and widespread, but in the end and to satisfy her own curiosity to find out how true the gossip was so her interest in him developed. The truth in the rumours circulating about him should have been sufficient to warn her off even though Megan held back in spite of his persistent efforts to attract her to him. However, the woman in her with an inner core wanting her to consider the truth of the rumours decided to take up the challenge, but would she have the strength to be strong enough against such a good-looking foreman who at a young age had good prospects for the future?

Would this be a challenge she could not refuse? However curious she appeared commonsense prevailed and she decided not to become one of his trophies and add to the collection of his works' female personnel. Even if he really wanted her she decided not to give any help or encouragement, but the more she considered ignoring him the greater became his interest in her but Megan still said if he wanted her badly enough he would have to fight and prove worthy of the privilege of arousing her to respond to him, even though she did not make it easy for him and never gave him a direct answer or acknowledged his approaches by even the turn of the head. She knew this, coupled with the knowledge he was now becoming the subject of shopfloor speculation about her, was sapping his confidence more than anything else. One of the shopfloor girls altered the words of a well-known poem so he could regain his confidence;

'Oh to be in England now that April's there'

to

'Oh to be at work now that Andrew's here.'

He would look out when Megan finished work in the evening, but if she caught sight of him first would hurry away making sure he knew she had seen him. In the works he had official contact through her to the managing director, but she was easily able to cope with him, and would not allow him to deviate from works' business, or she ignored any personal questions he directed at her. If he had to wait to see the managing director she would give him a cup of tea. It was puzzling for Andrew to be put on the defensive and have to admit what had been a successful and unchanged technique of long standing did not work. It jolted his confidence and he had no immediate answer. Megan had the impression he had decided to change his tactics and concentrate on her.

She realised she was beginning to win by her seemingly *laissez-faire* attitude. Her intention had not been so much to remove the opposition as to provide him with an alternative kind of date. It made heavy going for both of them, and when he thought he was winning so she would trip him up and he would have to start over again. The thought of losing her made him try all the harder. He had not taken into account that she had set her course and would not be diverted by the method he always considered the most successful. It would have been so much easier if he had accepted from the beginning that there was no way he could get away with a temporary choice and change it to suit himself. It would be a lasting relationship or nothing.

The pursuit by Andrew of Megan was one of the most talked of subjects by the works' and office staff. It was not difficult to understand why the other girls would not give up their claim on him, but if they were honest with themselves they knew they were non-starters once he took an interest in Megan. After the best part of a year and with no solution forthcoming the managing director intervened on Andrew's behalf otherwise the production would suffer. His intervention proved to be successful.

The courtship and marriage which followed, and Megan

becoming part of a big family, could not have been more pleasing than to Rhys who had worked hard behind the scenes to help it to come about. Megan did all she could to make the marriage work. She was home before him to prepare the evening meal. The first few years were marvellous with plenty to do inside and outside of the house. Megan noticed Andrew seemed to become easily distracted and she remembered his reputation with other women and the start of frequent rows they were beginning to have. She knew he was trying hard to put down the past, but because of his nature he could not always control his feelings. A stronger character could have shrugged it off.

It was not that Megan was cold towards him so much as Andrew not being able to understand the difference between Megan who wanted love and not the sex he considered would not make any different to the shopfloor girls. It was inevitable the coldness developing between them caused frustration and bad temper. She knew he had spoken to Rhys about their problem and it seemed to make things better between them. Rhys started to call to see them to make sure everything was all right. She liked him and responded like a sister. She knew all about his war record and a trust built up and they were able to talk more freely. Andrew would see them walking down the garden deep in conversation and knew he was the subject of their talk. Megan would listen to Rhys as they walked down the garden and knew he was trying to tell her not so much about the facts of life, but some of the flaws in Andrew without it being seen he was decrying Andrew.

Megan on thinking back realised Rhys had without the slightest hint of criticism of either of them shown her the way forward not so much to save their marriage, but ensure the happiness both of them were after. When Rhys died she missed him as much as any member of the family and there are still occasions when he would come flooding back into her thoughts. Andrew never fully knew how much he had contributed to their marriage. Megan said to Llewellyn, 'Why did it have to be Rhys who died?'

Her plan of action started on the Saturday night out with the family and instead of having her usual soft drinks, she drank whiskies, but not too many. Andrew noticed this but said nothing. To Megan it was one of the best Saturdays for a long time. They chatted and laughed together all the way home in the car. She made a cup of coffee for each of them in the kitchen when they arrived home. Andrew kept looking at her and wondered if she would give him an explanation, but there was complete silence. Andrew when he finished his coffee locked the doors while Megan washed the cups. He wondered why there was such a change in her and it made him apprehensive.

Megan took a long time to undress, and to Andrew it seemed as though he had been in bed for ages. He could not understand what was happening, and felt strange and unsure of himself. All he knew was that he loved and wanted Megan. Andrew for the first time ever realised Megan would always be his first consideration, and for the once as they made love held back so they both achieved a unison of climax. They both felt the turmoil and past resentments leaving them as they laid side by side.

As she laid quietly by the side of Andrew recovering from the passion of their love-making she was hoping she would never again have to worry over Andrew's transgressions.

On the Sunday Andrew kept looking at her and she would lower her head and could feel herself blushing all over. He would walk towards her and hold her at arms' length as though he was afraid of losing her. She remembered Rhys once saying to her, 'Megan, there may be events and/or occasions that to some people would satisfy their needs, but there is nothing so wonderous as the physical expression of true love between two people who equally care for each other.' Poor Andrew had always thought four pints of beer and a weekly jump was the answer.

MEGAN SAID TO LLEWELLYN,

'Why did it have to be Rhys who died?'

THE PARADE

Llewellyn could see the officer commanding the parade walking across to speak to the RSM and at the same time could see the four army cadets who were carrying out sentinel duty on each corner of the Cenotaph stood absolutely still and resolute, but looked very cold. The band was playing quietly as the wreath bearers fell out and at the same time a collection for the British Legion Poppy Fund was taking place.

As Llewellyn stood with all the other wreath bearers he glanced down at the names on his wreath:

DAD   1st WORLD WAR (DEAD)
GARETH 2nd WORLD WAR (KILLED AT NORMANDY)
JOHN   2nd WORLD WAR (DEAD)
RHYS   2nd WORLD WAR (DEAD)

The RSM stood ready to make his next command,

AVRIL SAID TO LLEWELLYN,

*'It is a pity I cannot choose relatives
like I do friends.'*

AVRIL SAID TO LLEWELLYN,

'It is a pity I cannot choose relatives like I do friends.'

AVRIL. She is the youngest of the family and as with Andrew the intervention of the war which moved the family to their dad's place of work gave her a difficult start to life, but not so much that there were friends left behind when they left, as she was too young, but more so because most of the older members of the family were in the army. She probably never realised she had older brothers. She was a pretty child and liked by everyone. She was never greedy or self-centred, and that was the reason why a fuss was always made of her. Avril had the ability to learn a song quickly and had a nice singing voice. She was good at swimming and became a member of the school swimming team, and eventually captain.

Her eventual problem was her initial inability to grasp subjects like maths, spelling and English. When she left school she obtained an office job and after a lot of hard work taught herself to type and became a secretary to one of the managers at the council offices. She became discontented with her way of life and showed a side of herself not noticed before and became depressed and moody. It was woe betide anyone who upset her, especially her mam and dad. Coupled with a newly discovered selfish streak, her daily tantrums caused the family to remind her how difficult she had become, but she would only retaliate. So it was best to leave her until she cooled off. It was difficult trying to find out what was wrong and when the family attempted to do so she would say she had got into the habit of having to fend for herself and could not now get used to so many of the family around her.

A strange quirk she had was not to look a person straight in the face when talking to them and it took a long time before she had sufficient confidence in herself to lose the habit. With strangers she could be absolutely charming. She must have regretted not involving herself more with the family, but with some wisdom also she would often say, 'It is a pity I cannot chose my relatives like I do my friends'. By this time she was a presentable person, but still difficult with the family. She knew what clothes to wear and they were usually new.

Avril should have been proud of her brothers and to be pleasant to them instead of to outsiders, as most members of big families normally are. This was a start of an unhappy life ahead of her not that it would show on her face, or that she would ever say why. She made her mind up very early she would only marry a person who measured up to her idea of someone who would provide the material requirements of life rather than a loving atmosphere and at the same time unwittingly or otherwise accept her as the dominant partner. One felt she would provide the life her husband would want insomuch as sex would be available as an added means to achieve the lifestyle she wanted but it would not be an obvious ploy. Her one fear was if her partner thought her need for sex would exceed his, but her active participation was more of a loving gesture than simply sex.

She grew into a good-looking young woman and was not short of boyfriends, but made up her mind she was not going to be an excuse for others to find out the facts of life. The slightest attempt by any of the boys she went out with to put her into a compromising position left him with her hand on his face or even her knee in his groin. It was strange to think her body was her only asset. It could be thought that only older women had those thoughts, not a young girl.

Avril always searched for security from an early age. Even her pocket money was saved at the end of each week. To ask her for a loan until the end of the week would be a sheer waste of time. It was difficult to understand why money took priority over all other family involvements. Eventually she met Ivor who had completed his National Service in the Welsh Fusiliers and lived near her home. To others he did not seem to fit into her plans for the future, but Avril is not known for making mistakes when it concerns her interests. From the beginning of their courtship he may not have seen her in her proper light, or perhaps he may have also seen what he was looking for as his future partner.

Ivor fared no better than the rest of her previous boyfriends when it came to trying to go further than the kissing stage. The prize to him was always tantalizingly near and thought her innocence to his ever-growing need was her chance of netting the fish.

Ivor was as careful with money as Avril, so her perception in her evaluation of him was to her credit. She was not in any way pleased with his work as a rough painter for a large contract painting firm, but there were opportunities for quick promotion.

Avril knew it would not take long for him to get his first step on the ladder and within six months he became a foreman of the outside painting gang. It was difficult for him as he was distrusted by the older men and only by bullying the younger members of the gang was he able to meet the contract target times.

Her mam and dad liked him because Avril would be on her best behaviour whenever he went to the house. When they became engaged she insisted on the most expensive engagement ring and an engagement party at the best local hotel. Her poor dad was landed with the engagement party bill. At the party they both said they only wanted a short engagement and they tentatively named April as the month for the wedding, which was six months away. Preparations went ahead and Avril again insisted on the best hotel for the reception. Dress would be formal for the main guests.

Avril and Ivor were by this time seeing each other most evenings and regularly went to her mam's for tea on Sunday. As the wedding date drew nearer so they were finding themselves in compromisingly loving situations and becoming more difficult for her to hold back his desire for her. Each time they became worked up so she wanted sex as much as him, but would still hold back, not that she was concerned with losing her virginity, as it was only a word. It was security she was after, and if allowing him sex was the means to achieve this aim he could have full use of her body. With the wedding so near she fully expected Ivor to make a move, and without any objection from her in fully participating in sex, but Avril wanted to be sure it was her decision, and not his, but he never made the obvious move.

Avril knew what she wanted and the cost to others did not figure into the pattern of events for the future as she was able to blot out anything unpleasant. Neither Ivor nor the rest of the family knew the full cost in happiness she lost or what it did to her peace of mind.

Avril's wedding was an event of some importance as Ivor had invited all his family. They set out it seemed to impress all with their money and property and it appeared to be the subject of their conversation whenever the opportunity arose. The main guests wore morning suits. The reception was held at the best local hotel and the arrangements were first-class. The wedding couple set off for their honeymoon from Rhoose airport bound for Salou in Spain. Some of the guests saw them off. After a quick change most of the guests decided to make a night of it at the local pub where a room had been booked and a buffet laid on. Ivor's relatives were asked if they would like to attend. They were so pleased with the invitation they not only offered to pay for the buffet but would not take no for an answer. It was a marvellous night and they all finished up at Avril's mam's house to round the occasion off. They did not break up until about three in the morning. Their appreciative behaviour gave Llewellyn food for thought, and realised they were not trying to impress anyone, but were genuinely nice people.

It took a long time for her to settle down to married life. Avril asked Rhys to come and see their new house. He never mentioned to her that Ivor had spoken to him about her shouting at him for no obvious reason. He asked in a roundabout way if things were all right between her and Ivor. She told him Ivor was asking her to account for how she was spending the housekeeping money. This surprised Rhys, knowing how careful she was with money.

Rhys again spoke to Ivor who gave a different reason for their difficulties, but was most reluctant to elaborate any further. This state of affairs went on for months until Rhys was brought into it again. This time he asked Avril in no uncertain manner what was wrong between them. With her head down she said Ivor was making unreasonable demands upon her. So it was back to Ivor and Rhys said unless he started telling him the truth about what was wrong between him and Avril he would find his teeth down the back of his throat. Ivor was tempted to tell Rhys to mind his own business, but when he saw the look in Rhys's eyes he suddenly felt afraid of him.

Rhys held him by his coat collar and pulled him until he saw the look on Rhys's face and then he quickly told him that she ignored him in bed and had done so for a few months. Rhys let go of his collar and asked what sort of man he was not to be able to put their problems behind them without involving others. Rhys walked away without another word. Ivor never forgot the look Rhys gave him and Avril only had to mention the name Rhys to see the colour draining from his face. At least it did them a lot of good and they settled down to married life without any further trouble. Avril became very competent at looking after their money and Ivor was grateful later on in life that she was so good.

As the years went by Avril slowly stopped seeing her mam and dad as those barriers put up as a teenager began to reappear, and it became a saying of hers that its a pity I cannot chose my relatives like I do my friends, but she had no peace of mind and probably had pangs of remorse.

Avril said little when she heard her eldest brother had died in Australia. She and Ivor settled their differences over money. She found he would have unreasonable moods, and thought it was her fault and the only way she could bring him round was to put her arms around him and kiss him until she felt him responding to her and he would lower her to the floor and make love.

Avril still worried about money and however much she saved was afraid it would stop and started to feel insecure. The family said that however much money she had it would never be enough and it was a worry she would have for the rest of her life, or was she more contented than others realised.

As they were beginning to settle down her dad died. She could not accept what had happened and even when Rhys called he could not reconcile her to the fact. When she looked at Rhys she realised how ill he looked, but was afraid to ask him how he was. Rhys looked at her and for a fleeting moment accepted there were a lot of his characteristics in her and this seemed to bridge a gap between them.

During the early years after her dad died she again distanced herself from the rest of the family. She was pleased Ivor was making good progress at work and had told Avril he now had sufficient experience of painting to start his own business. She had three lovely children and with the business doing so well they again moved and she never seemed happier. Having a nice big house helped.

When she found out Rhys was attending hospital regularly she went and visited him, but only on the one occasion and never went again. Rhys understood her reason and accepted it which removed some of the guilt she felt. She never saw Rhys alive again, and inwardly mourned him.

AVRIL SAID TO LLEWELLYN,

'It is a pity I cannot chose relatives like I do friends.'

THE PARADE

The RSM with the dignity of the occasion quietly asked the wreath bearers to make a line ready for the wreath laying ceremony. Each followed the other and waited in turn as each wreath was laid and with two steps backwards acknowledged the event with a pause or a salute. This went on until all the wreaths were laid.

The last wreath was laid by a woman in her thirties. She was hardly able to step back because she was overcome with emotion during her silent prayer. By this time she was being observed by many of those attending. As she walked from the Cenotaph with tears streaming down her face there was an older person waiting for her and as she started to hurry towards him he was just able to catch her as she collapsed in his arms. The wreath bearers and poppy sellers returned to the ranks.

To most ex-service personnel and dependants the parade is not only the occasion for wearing medals, but an obligation to those no longer with us, and as we know we would have been equally remembered by them. Llewellyn hoped this form of remembrance would be carried on in perpetuity, and as the world is getting smaller by the collapsing of borders this homage could include those we fought against.

IVOR SAID TO LLEWELLYN,

'Ask Avril to stop shouting at me.'

IVOR SAID TO LLEWELLYN,

'Ask Avril to stop shouting at me.'

IVOR. Llewellyn never knew Ivor until he started seeing Avril and found it difficult entering into a conversation with him as he would limit his remarks to material things such as property, cars and money, fairly heavy subjects for a young man to be talking about on their first meeting. Avril thought he was marvellous and it must have hurt her that the family had little respect for his monetary outlook. It did not appear to him that family life could be an important part of his life.

He was not afraid of hard work providing it was to his advantage. He was employed as a rough painter, which to him was the same as labouring, but the wages were good even though it was dirty work and long hours. He saw the potential of promotion to foreman and lost little time in making sure he caught the manager's eye when he did his rounds to answer any questions put to the painting gang.

It was after he returned from doing his National Service in the Infantry that he was able to get the painting job. He worked hard and instinctively knew he was on his way up, but was not the least distressed that the other members of the painting gang did not trust him.

Ivor met Avril after he started work as a painter and they saw each other regularly. It was evident she saw in him a person who would be a good provider and if making money and acquiring possessions were important then he was her man. He saw in Avril a very beautiful young woman who would be an asset equally necessary for all he considered important. Life was not easy as he had been limited to the work he could obtain because he only had a primary education. He worked hard as a painter and his aim was to become a foreman in order to be able to learn the other side of the business. He accepted that having to creep was a small price to pay. He lost the respect of his fellow painters, but did achieve his aim to become a foreman. He did not consider going to a technical college to learn the commercial aspect of the work. Ivor had sufficient confidence in himself to make money without any distractions.

Ivor enjoyed Avril's family as his family were a lot older and set in their ways, but his obvious approach of taking and not giving quickly meant they stopped asking him to join their company when out. It never occurred to him he had to pay his share when in a group night out. Slowly but surely he ended up with his own company unless Avril was with him. He never became a real friend of the brothers and in the end an invisible door was shut against him and once he married Avril they saw little of him afterwards, unless he wanted something.

Most of the problems between Ivor and Avril were usually brought about by his meanness and a trait in his make-up which in later life cost him the comfort and protection of her family. To Ivor their marriage was part of his long-term plan to better himself whatever the cost to others. What he could not complain about was how Avril's family made sure she had the best possible on her wedding day.

Ivor had a preoccupation with sex which was with him throughout their courtship, and he would use any opportunity to take his chances and for Avril there was no way she could hold him back short of finishing with him. Her attempts to grip his manhood and stimulate the sex act only acted to delay what he wanted. It was like money – he only thought that having all of her for himself would satisfy him.

Ivor certainly made it to a foreman, but through hard work and a loss of self-esteem. His next goal was to start his own business and during his time as a foreman he made sure he knew all the clients of his employer and how he compiled his estimates for the price of a contract. He kept records of all the suppliers of materials and the costs. Ivor knew he could only initially win a contract once he started on his own by his contract price being less than the competitors.

Once he started his firm he did find it difficult getting contracts, but having prior knowledge of a competitor's quotation enabled Ivor to undercut his price. He built up a good painting crew and was shrewd enough to employ a working chargehand who was a time-served painter with a good technical knowledge. The rest of the crew were young men with little or no painting experience. Ivor was a good employer, but expected his men to work hard and work overtime. In order for contracts to be finished on time he introduced incentive payments for employees based on a share of the money saved on finishing the contract early. The painting crews would be issued with a start and finish time for the contract and if the time was beaten they would share the difference. This proved to be a winner, but eventually they cut their own throats by cutting corners and Ivor received complaints from his clients. He changed the method of incentive payments to running total over a period of six months and any poor workmanship would have to be rectified with no incentive payment, which had the effect of reducing the overall share with the resultant money correction.

Ivor never achieved a reputation for good workmanship as it was necessary to undercut the quotations of his competitors. He diversified his work to include steel erection and sheeting (cladding) of new and old buildings and again undercut all his competitors and was never short of work. He tried hard to be liked, but his overriding obsession with making money deterred this and his inability to mix did not help, coupled with his not being trusted. One of his sayings was that there is no such thing as family where business was concerned and as he expanded he saw less of Avril's relatives. Most of the family knew it would happen when it suited him, not that they would not miss him. Unfortunately, it also meant they saw less of Avril.

Whenever Ivor saw Rhys and could not avoid him he was unsure of himself but always thought Rhys would make a good partner as the total success of any business needed at least one of the partners who had some standing in the community, and Rhys was such a person. Ivor wanted someone who he could share his success with, but his reluctance was because he was afraid that any obviously visual move would be considered a sign of weakness on his part, or that people would take advantage of him, but he was beginning to win over his clients by good quality workmanship.

The business made remarkable progress and with the

introduction of steel erection and sheeting he was never short of orders so he decided to add the fabrication of portable building in order to keep abreast of his competitors. The new line proved to add stability to his business and as it divorced him more from the shopfloor into the commercial side he started worrying by not being directly involved with the production side if target dates would not be met.

By this time Avril had three children and was becoming less involved with the running of the office side of the business. They again moved, this time to a large detached house with sufficient land to keep for future speculation. She had learned to drive and Ivor bought her a car, not that she made use of it to visit her mam and dad as she said there was never enough time for visits.

Ivor and Avril had many more rows as the business progressed, and she could not wait until the children were old enough for her to return to a more active part in the business.

IVOR SAID TO LLEWELLYN,

'Ask Avril to stop shouting at me.'

THE PARADE

When the parade settled down after the wreath-laying ceremony they all awaited the solemn act of Remembrance by the chaplain and after the prayers and responses were made they all said the Lord's Prayer.

> Our Father who art in Heaven,
> Hallowed be thy Name,
> Thy Kingdom Come,
> Thy will be done,
> On earth as it is in Heaven,
> Give us this day our daily bread,
> And forgive us our trespasses,
> As we forgive those who trespass against us,
> And lead us not into temptation,
> But deliver us from evil,
> For Thine is the Kingdom,
> The Power and the Glory,
> For ever and ever,
> Amen.

The officer commanding the parade then said:

> They shall not grow old, as we that are left grow old:
> Age shall not weary them, nor the years condemn.
> At the going down of the sun and in the morning
> We will remember them.
>
> We will remember them.

Llewellyn saw Phillip was deep in thought and wondered if he was thinking of the comrades he had lost during the war, and he was looking at the name Gareth on the Cenotaph. Gareth was the first one of the Edwards' family to die through direct enemy action.

SIAN SAID TO LLEWELLYN,

'I have asked Mam to live with me.'

75

SIAN SAID TO LLEWELLYN,

'I have asked Mam to live with me.'

SIAN was the oldest daughter and because her mam was working part-time had from an early age been told to do most of the housework and also the shopping, including making sure the younger children left for school on time and looking after them during the school holidays. It was a rush preparing breakfast for them and getting herself ready for school. Her mam would prepare the evening meal. Her dad worked nights and would be asleep most afternoons and early evenings. During the week-end she would help him with the large garden.

Sian was popular with the other girls at school and being above average height she stood out against the other girls. This helped her to develop leadership qualities. She was certainly the favourite of her dad. They went to chapel together and when he played bowls at the local park she would watch from the side of the green. She would always sit near him when he played the piano and when he sang it always seemed as though he was singing to her.

They had a good father and daughter relationship throughout the years until his death. It was strange Avril never wanted to be near her dad and preferred her mam. When the four brothers were called up in 1939 it put a lot of extra work on her young shoulders. Her two brothers, Owen and Andrew, were little help to her, but Owen had a job taking milk around before and after school. He was able to bring home vegetables from the farm, and they were a help.

Sian was bright at school and able to learn easily. She took part in school concerts and entered most of the events on sports day. When the colliery where her dad worked closed down shortly after the war started he was sent to a large works some miles away and after some months was allocated a fairly new semi-detached house. It took some time for her to settle down, but once she made new friends it was as if she had always lived there. At the new school she had better opportunities to continue her athletic interests. The sports teacher noticed she was above average and offered to coach her. She was picked to run not only for the school but also for the county and won numerous trophies. Her picture, so we are told, still hangs in the main hall of the school with some of her cups and medals.

Sian more than any of the family missed being part of a large family when her brothers were away as she was growing into a young woman, and would have liked the unofficial protection of them.

The American soldiers were stationed near their home, but had little to do with the local people. Sian would never go near the camp unless with another girl and even then would run past the entrance to the camp. If one of the soldiers shouted after them they would be gone like a flash. The soldiers eventually left to take part in the Normandy Landings, but they were missed by the local people.

Sian was growing into a very pretty teenager and received more than a glance from local boys. Andrew was now able to look after himself, so it gave Sian more time for herself, but Avril was too young to be left on her own. Once the three brothers were demobbed Sian obtained employment as an office girl at a local transport firm. She was not sorry to leave school as the new job gave her some independence which she never had before and with the pocket money from her wages she was able to buy clothes of her own choice.

She started to go around with girls from the office, but still had little to do with boys. Her track running was neglected and her coach was disappointed, but accepted that the school and country representation had been as much for them as herself and with the display cabinet of her cups and medals they were truly pleased.

Sian worried about her dad's health and the long hours he worked did little to help. Not that he ever gained his full health from the time he was a POW during the First World War, but like Sian he was pleased to see three of his sons home. Sian and her dad were alike, and not only in appearance. They had similar mannerisms and a shyness which meant they never forced themselves on others. Both were definitely careful with money.

Sian and Glenys became good friends even though there were a few years difference in their age. There was a young man recently returned form the army who was employed as a fitter where she worked. He fancied her and always had a reason to make a visit to her office. He eventually plucked up the courage to ask her for a date. What Sian did not know was that her dad and Phillip regularly played skittles for the same team, so it meant they had a common interest.

Sian and Phillip decided to get married within a few months and Rhys was asked to be the best man. Owen was unable to attend the wedding because he was still in Germany with the RAF. It was a warm and sunny day for the wedding. Her dad was nervous so Sian gave him some whisky before the wedding car arrived. They were a few minutes late getting to the church, but once in the church with the organ playing as her and her dad walked down the aisle their nerves calmed down. They certainly looked a very good couple and at the reception they only had eyes for each other. The church hall where they held their reception was packed with all the relatives of both families.

The photographer forgot to turn up at the church to take the photos and one of the family went to fetch him, so they decided to go ahead with the reception and take the photos afterwards. When he arrived they all trooped outside for the photo taking.

Sian said her mam and dad spared no expense with the wedding in spite of the shortages and the cost of everything, including the hire of the cars. The families helped to ensure there was plenty to eat. There was a shortage of sherry and port so without the guests knowing both the wines were diluted with lemonade. It resulted in the women drinking more and they were soon affected by the extra drinks.

Once the honeymoon couple left things went flat, so they all decided to tidy up the church hall and pack away the glass, chinaware and cutlery. Most of the family and guests started to prepare the buffet for the evening and the men packed it into boxes to take to the local hotel where a room had been booked. Within an hour all those who loaned glasses etc had claimed them and the church hall was locked. There were more people attending the buffet, but there was plenty for everybody and by closing time they all said what a wonderful day and evening they had had.

When the honeymoon couple returned the family met them at the railway station and when asked how they enjoyed themselves they almost hardly answered them. They moved straight into rented rooms a few streets away and Sian said afterwards it was strange only being two after coming from a large family.

Llewellyn and Rhys saw Phillip regularly for skittle matches and he always appeared to be miserable. This went on for some time until Phillip mentioned to Rhys in a vague sort of way that their lovemaking was not what it should be and if he started to make love to Sian she would freeze up and the harder he tried the more she held back. He said there was no way he could make any progress and if he tried to remove any of her clothes she would grip his hands so tightly and short of using physical strength to overcome her resistance there was nothing he could do so it was off to sleep.

Phillip asked what he should do, and it ended up with him and Rhys sitting down together. Llewellyn tried to listen but apart from the word 'gin' he was unable to hear what they were saying. Anyrate the substance of the problem was Sian because of her inability to relax when she and Phillip tried to make love. Eventually and after he and Rhys had a few more chats together it seemed as though they had arrived at a solution.

A few weeks afterwards, and when they saw Phillip again he looked as pleased as punch, so naturally Llewellyn called to see Sian, but apart from being more than her usual self she said nothing else. The reluctance of both of them to say any more about it gave it all the ingredients of an unsolved crime (of passion). Many months later Glenys inadvertently mentioned it to Llewellyn, not realising he knew nothing about how it all ended nor how it started.

What had been the subject of discussion between Phillip and Rhys started with Phillip asking Sian if she would like to go out for dinner. A restaurant was agreed between them and a date. When the day arrived Sian wondered what the occasion was. Everything went according to plan and both sat down in the restaurant, having a drink while their meal was being prepared. Phillip had orderd a sweet sherry for Sian and whisky for himself. When the meal was ready and they sat down Phillip ordered a bottle of white wine and he made sure her glass was topped up all the time. After the meal they went into the lounge for coffee. When Phillip ordered the drinks he looked at Sian and she made no objection to his selection of gin and bitter lemon for the both of them. There was no slowing down of drinks and Sian started to giggle and more sips of her gin and bitter lemons increased the giggling. Phillip then realised it was time to leave.

Sian did riot seem to have a care in the world, but she needed some guiding to the car. When they arrived home Sian decided to open the front door as Phillip put the car in the garage. When he got to the front door she was still struggling to open the front door and when she eventually unlocked it she made straight upstairs to the bedroom, and almost without any signs of modesty undressed, and into her pyjamas, and after a quick visit to the bathroom got straight into bed, and curled over on her side and was asleep in a few seconds. Phillip was still undressing himself, and as he climbed into the bed he felt her turning towards him and she responded in a positive manner to him.

Afterwards Phillip thought to himself what good advice Rhys had given him and also realised there would be no future difficulties between him and Sian.

When Sian next saw Rhys she thought how ill he looked, but knew he would not thank her if she mentioned it to him. During this time she regularly corresponded with John in Australia and in one of his letters he said he was bringing over his family for a holiday, and his wife and children would spend most of it in Scotland with her parents.

Sian made arrangements for him to spend time with his mam and other members of the family. John enjoyed his stay and when Catherine came down from Scotland with the children for the last few days they were all pleased to see them. Within a few days they were on the way back to Australia.

Sian had a funny feeling she would not see John again and the thought nagged her for a long time. To Sian it was the same look on his face she was seeing whenever she saw Rhys. It was as if both of them were running parallel with what the war had cost them. Sian never confided her fear to anyone. Shortly afterwards she had a letter from John saying they were all returning home once they sold the farm and would live in Scotland near Catherine's family. At least, she thought to herself, Scotland was a lot nearer than Australia. It was not to be as John died a few days before the journey home.

Sian found herself spending more time with her mam as she was finding it difficult looking after herself. Eventually her mam asked if she could come and live with her and she told Llewellyn what her mam had said.

Sian gave birth over the intervening years, to a boy first and later a girl. They decided to put a deposit on a terraced house in the village not too far from where Phillip worked. When the children were old enough to look after themselves Sian went back to work. During this time Rhys had married and Andrew started courting. With Avril married and moved away from the village it certainly made life easier for her mam.

When their mam and dad returned from their holidays with Glenys and Llewellyn Sian was told her dad had not been well during his holiday. A few weeks later he went into hospital and a few weeks later died. On the last days before he died it was only Sian and Rhys he wanted to visit him and they both were with him when he died. Even though the three of them were in deep conversation right up to the end none of the family were told what was said between them.

Sian asked Phillip if he would take Rhys up to the hospital for treatment and wait for him. As the treatment developed so Rhys had to stay in for longer periods and he stayed in until his eventual demise. Sian felt the loss more than the rest of the family as he was her favourite brother.

The effect on their mam of the death of Rhys was long-drawn-out and her health declined more rapidly and it would only be a question of time before she moved in with Sian.

Sian arranged the sale of the house soon after their mam moved in with her. Initially there were problems, but they became less once their mam accepted it was as much her home as her previous house. With the care and attention she received, and with the doctor calling regularly to check her health and nothing stinted to ensure this, all her brothers and other sister realised she could not be in better hands.

SIAN SAID TO LLEWELLYN,

'I have asked Mam to live with me.'

THE PARADE

As the response finished with 'We will remember them' so did the RSM shout the next command.

'PARADE, PARADE SHUN',

and this was proceeded by a single bandsman playing 'The Last Post' followed by The Silence. During the silence Llewellyn could only think of the names of comrades no longer with them and as the places, incidents and dates crowded his mind the bandsman stopped playing.

When the reveille finished there was a change in the mood of those attending the Remembrance service.

SIAN SAID TO LLEWELLYN,

'Phillip has gone out for petrol.'

SIAN SAID TO LLEWELLYN,

'Phillip has gone out for petrol.'

PHILLIP. Llewellyn did not know Phillip Williams until after Sian brought him home to meet her mam and dad. He quickly became a favourite with the whole family, especially their mam because he was considerate and helpful and nothing was too much trouble. Being a fitter, he was able to turn his hand to most things. One person who had the benefit from this was Rhys because whatever car he bought always had something wrong with it and Phillip would be asked to look at it.

Rhys never took advantage of Phillip and the family felt their personal friendship benefited from a respect for the other's service record.

As a foreman and an apprentice trained tradesman, he was always in demand. Most evenings after work he would have a caller wanting him to look at his car and also having a good working knowledge of electrical housework kept him busy. Sian was appreciative of the extra money it brought in.

For all that Phillip was painfully shy and preferred to stay in the background, Sian's mam and dad saw something special in him. From the word go he was the ideal partner for Sian and she knew it and it was proved so over and over again.

Llewellyn knew nothing of his war service other than he spent most of it overseas on specialist communication duties. He was called up early in 1940 and having a first class brain, was quick to learn. This gave him promotion to the highest non-commissioned rank of regimental sergeant-major. He was given the opportunity to take a course as a preparatory requirement to being considered for a commission, but did not proceed with it.

Over the years, and with the little information gleaned from different sources, it would appear he was involved with work behind enemy lines on detection of troop movement, but anymore than that has been impossible to find out, short of asking him and even then it was probable he would not say.

He and other members of his section had been given specialist training which included written examinations in order to confirm if they had the ability to undertake the duties involved. It was said the failure rate was very high. His commanding officer was disappointed when Phillip refused to have his name put forward for a commission but, as he said to the OC, he would get more out of the men as an NCO than as an officer. His OC accepted this explanation.

Phillip was liked by the officers and the men in the specialist group. His natural ability to absorb information and the intricate working of the equipment used brought out his leadership qualities. The men trusted him to deal with all situations and the officers never had to worry about the orders they passed on to him. If he had a weakness it was that he did not appear to know if he was being taken for a ride or taken advantage of. Perhaps this was the basis of his success with people, or the penalty for accepting their trust come what may. However Phillip did have the strength of character to accept that not everything is perfect and that allowances have to be made.

The war was not easy for him, and it is worth remembering he was only twenty years of age when he joined up. He was demobbed in 1946, having spent over four years overseas. It took a long time for him to settle down, but he found no difficulty in restarting work, although as he had not finished his apprenticeship he had another year to complete it. Phillip was not long in being promoted to foreman in the transport and maintenance department.

Phillip met Sian at their works' canteen during the lunch break and was immediately attracted to her and in spite of his shy nature quickly established a talking relationship with her. He always made sure he would sit on her table or near to it. When he asked her for a date he blurted it out and started to blush. What he did not know was that she had been waiting for a long time for him to ask her out. He became a regular visitor to her house. Their dates were usually walks, sometimes the pictures and sometimes for a drink.

His health was not good and after a visit to the hospital the doctor told him to take it easy for the next three months. Like most ex-servicemen he had a morbid fear of hospitals and no amount of reassurance by others would change his views.

They were married in 1949, and spent their honeymoon at a small hotel in Hereford. Even by looking at Phillip one could see how much he loved her. Even if she only hinted she liked something, by the next time they met he would have bought it for her.

During their honeymoon and for a long time aftewards, their love-making was a complete disaster. However hard he tried with Sian he only had limited cooperation in trying to make love and was able to go so far and no further. Phillip thought her innocence or reluctance was incomprehensible, considering that she was from a large family where children learn the facts of life very young.

Phillip said she never lost her shyness or look of innocence and anything smutty would easily upset her. He also thought he had a lot to thank Rhys for his suggestions. He recognised the need to accept the strength and weaknesses of them both and to preserve it if they were to have a happy and normal married life.

He quickly moved into a managerial position and again attributed his promotion to the acceptance of the weaknesses as well as the strength of those in his charge, although he never expressed these views and strived to bring out their better features.

John had left for Australia some months before they were married and knew little about the oldest brother, but they became great friends when John returned for a holiday some years after.

Both William and Olwen were growing up, and without any doubt were a credit to Sian and Phillip. They would whenever possible join the family Saturday night out and it would be his job to look after the kitty. Rhys and Phillip always sat together and would drink pint for pint. Considering that one trusted everyone until he found out otherwise, so Rhys was the opposite and trusted no one outside the family and even if he spent time in their company it still made no difference. The family put it down to the experience he encountered when fighting with the Ghurkas against the Japanese in Burma.

One of the best weddings attended by everyone was Gwen and Rhys's and for a man who trusted so few the buffet at the local pub in the evening was packed.

The firm Phillip worked for was expanding rapidly to cater

for the post-war boom and the demand for all forms of transport vehicles kept him away from home for long periods. It was not to his liking, but he realised the need for him to keep abreast of the competition.

He was shortly afterwards promoted to works' manager. The responsibility and authority was well within his capability and with an increase in salary including a company car which resolved his personal transport problems he decided to let Sian have his own car.

He found he had less time to himself and had to make an appearance at the works most week-ends if only for a few hours. One of his first tasks after his own promotion was to pick someone to take over his old position. His technical knowledge on transport was certainly put to use and he quickly started looking for larger premises to accommodate the increased volume of work and to consider obtaining warehouse facilities, as the trend was not only to transport goods but also to store them.

In conjunction with the managing director he made a survey and was able to lease a large building with the option to purchase at a later date. The property belonged to the war department and was near the docks. It was ideal for their use as it included road and rail facilities with loading bays, office and canteen. They engaged a firm of civil engineers to modify the building and Phillip acted as liasion officer to monitor progress. Once the work was completed it was soon evident it would be a successful venture and again they had to consider further expansion and found it necessary to turn to the bank for capital to finance their requirements. Phillip was promoted to local director and allocated shares to enable him to attend board meetings and be able to voice his say formally.

On one of their nights out they noticed Avril with a young man sitting near them and asked them to join them. The four stayed together for the evening. He was introduced as Ivor who worked for a firm of painting contractors on the docks. Neither of them had much to say and it was left to Sian to do most of the talking.

Their new prosperity enabled them to buy a larger house some miles from the village and afterwards Sian took a part time job at the local sub post office. Phillip was not happy about her starting work as they did not need the money, but she said it was a long day for her as he worked long hours and with the children growing up she needed an added interest.

When John and Catherine and their children returned home from Australia for a holiday John stayed part of the time with Phillip and Catherine and the children went to Scotland.

Whenever Phillip was fortunate to have a Sunday morning away from work he would say to Sian about 12 o'clock that he was going for petrol, and would not be long, but it was nearer enough to 2 o'clock before he returned. Invariably he would see Rhys when he called in for a drink, and naturally they would end up talking about the war years.

Phillip has an uncomfortable feeling whenever he was with Rhys, who seemed to have a hidden mystical look in his eyes, which Phillip defined as not only sadness, but a fear he did not want to challange. Yet the feeling vanished when their eyes clashed and Rhys dispelled this and the fear with his wonderful smile, but his eyes remained cold.

Although Rhys' hands looked fragile and almost transparent, when he shook hands with Phillip his grip was still as hard as steel. Phillip had seen in Rhys the same undefined glimpse that Sian's mam had seen many years before. Rhys died six months later. Phillip to the present time never lost the feeling of hurt when he died and felt Rhys knew he was not long for this world.

Gareth was the brother killed in Normandy and Phillip had never met him and would often wonder why one of the favourite brothers, who had trained as a soldier for over four years as part of one of the finest regiments, and within less than one hour of landing on the beach in Normandy, was dead.

Phillip to Sian's mam and dad was a saint by his understanding and could never be more pleased that he joined the family.

SIAN SAID to LLEWELLYN,

'Phillip has gone out for petrol.'

THE PARADE

The RSM shouted the next command to the parade who had been standing to attention for the Silence.

'Parade. Parade stand at ease. Stand easy.'

This was a welcome relief to them. The Chaplain made his way to the microphone, and asked to turn to the last page of the hymn sheet, and he read out the first line of the hymn.

O God, our help in ages past.

The band started to play and those assembled began to sing,

O God, our help in ages past,
Our help for years to come,
Our shelter from the stormy blast,
And our eternal home.

and with the singing of the last line of the last verse,

And our eternal home,

Llewellyn at that moment could only think of his brothers no longer with him and their dad who would have enjoyed such an occasion.

OWEN SAID TO LLEWELLYN,

'I promise not to say you gave it to me.'

OWEN SAID TO LLEWELLYN,

'I promise not to say you gave it to me.'

OWEN was the fifth oldest son and next down to Rhys. For some reason or other he was always secretive and contrary to most of the brothers, in the sense that he kept even the most trivial things to himself. His different outlook and behaviour could partly be due to the four brothers being called up while he was still in his early teens and not having had them to confide and having had to use his own initiative and resources for most of his formative years.

As a boy he liked farm animals and spent a lot of his time on the farm and had a part-time job delivering milk before and after school and at week-ends. In the morning and evening he carried the milk in a can with a lid. It held two gallons. (Pre-war milk in bottles was the exception.) He would knock at the door of the customers, or they would leave a jug outside the back door. The amount ordered would be poured into a measure and tipped into the jug with a little extra for 'good measure'. But the only problem was it could mean a short measure for the last customer. Other reasons for not having enough milk was if Owen was stopped by the milk inspector who would ask for three samples of milk. One he handed back, one to be checked for water content and one sample he kept for himself. (He would pay for the milk taken.) It was hard work carrying the milk can from the farm to the village, then straight to school and after school back to the farm for a full can of milk and back to the village to deliver it to the customers. In the winter if he slipped on the icy road and spilled the milk, it was back to the farm for a refill.

It was not an easy life and he received 2/6 per week. (12½p in new money). The job Owen looked forward to was helping on

Friday night after milk and Saturday morning after milk with the farm labourer to sell fresh farm produce which was grown on the farm. Owen would knock at the customer's door and take the order, or the customer would come out to the horse and cart and select her own vegetables. The cart carried potatoes, cabbage, carrots, swedes, parsnips, onions, leeks, broad beans, peas and other vegetables depending on the time of year. The farmer also had his own round on a Friday and Saturday. Owen was paid an extra 2/6 for the vegetable round. He noticed when the farm labourer loaded both carts he would put the best vegetables on his own cart, and put extra sacks of potatoes and cabbages on his own cart without telling the farmer. At the end of the round on the Saturday afternoon the farm labourer would stop the horse and cart near the farm, and count the takings, and separate the money for the extra sacks of potatoes and cabbage he had put on his cart and he would give Owen 2/6 for himself and he would be given another 2/6 from the farmer for helping on the two days.

It was difficult for Owen to know what to do with the extra money, because if he gave it to his man she would be obliged to tell the farmer and it would then get the farm labourer in trouble so he used to hide the money. When the family moved at the beginning of the war Owen decided to give the extra money he had saved to his mam and it was a sum in excess of £45 and a fortune for the early years of the war, but she would not take it and told him to put it in a post office savings account. The money was never again mentioned between them.

Owen never had it easy during the war as he was too young to be called up. His dad worked long hours, and his mam had a part-time job so like, his oldest sister, he had to help with the housework. There were opportunities because of the shortage of manpower. Owen started work at a small engineering firm producing components for army tanks. He enjoyed the work, and with a quick brain, and a good pair of hands was able, after being taught, to operate a capstan lathe equipment to become very proficient, operating most of the metal cutting machines and he received top wages for his age. It was not a proper apprenticeship, but good enough to qualify him to quote the training he had been given, and it would count towards the granting of indentures.

Owen enjoyed the work as it gave him a good wage packet. His mam would only take money for board and lodgings but made him save the remainder less pocket money. He did this religiously every week, but the family never knew how much he was saving, or how much he had already saved. It would be a waste of time asking him for a loan as the answer would be no and to him there was no justifiable reason even to consider it. By the time the war was over he had saved a considerable sum of money, and when he was called up for the Royal Air Force for his National Service in 1946 he still regularly saved. He enjoyed the freedom of service life and spent eighteen months overseas. He never smoked and would use his free issue of cigarettes to barter for items of value.

During one of his leaves he got married, which was not part of his original plans for the future. It was a local girl whom he knew before he was called up. She was very good looking and it was easy to see why he was attracted to her. Jean would be an asset to his future plans.

Llewellyn was best men, and as Owen only had a seventy-two hours' pass things had to be done in a hurry and even though it was supposed to be a quiet wedding there was a good turn-out of relatives and friends and all had a marvellous time.

When Owen returned from his National Service he lived with Jean and her parents, but the arrangements did not suit Owen and Jean did not like the idea of sharing a kitchen with her mam as it was causing problems. Owen surprised out-siders when he paid cash for a 1938 semi-detached house with twenty acres of land on the side and rear of the house and abutting the main road. (The family were not surprised because he had been saving his money for over ten years.) He would not discuss his business affairs with the family and even Jean had no idea what his business intentions were, not that he kept Jean short of housekeeping money and gave extra whenever she wanted it.

He always bought good solid furniture, antique if possible, and would attend house clearance sales. Ornaments, and other small items he bought would not be considered if marked or damaged. However, he bought utility furniture with coupons because it was made to a high standard as imposed by the government, and always paying cash and made sure he had a discount from them. He had his sights firmly fixed to the future, that was to say *his* future. He was able to cultivate an acre of his land in the first year. It was hard work as he also worked full time and managed to repair and decorate the house.

There was a surplus of vegetables and flowers over and above their requirements and he decided to sell directly to the public at week-ends. He realised by the end of the season there was a good profit to be made and that people were prepared to spend on good garden produce. His second year's profit on trading directly to the public was extremely good and an improvement on the previous year. To cope Jean would serve the customers, but found it took too much of her time as she also had to look after their young child.

How he coped with a full time job, and expanded the land for cultivation was beyond comprehension and he was eventually forced by the sheer pressure of the work involved to hand in his notice at the engineering works. They were sorry to see him leave as he was such a good worker.

At the commencement of the third year he bought a badly damaged commercial greenhouse. He asked Rhys and Llewellyn to help him to prepare the base and erect it. They repaired the damaged woodwork and replaced broken panes of glass. The hardest job was repainting it, using a primitive scaffolding from scrap pipes and planks. But it was done to the satisfaction of Owen. It was then decided to install a coal heating system with hot water pipes around the inside of the greenhouse, fitted with a pump to circulate the hot water from an electric supply. Owen would have preferred paraffin but it was still in short supply. He used the greenhouse to bring on bedding plants and later grew tomatoes and shortly afterwards purchased another six acres of good agricultural land at the rear of the land he already owned, and within a few months bought another ten acres adjacent to his land. Both these parcels of land were considerably dearer than the first purchase and he concluded the deal with the option on another ten acres, making a total of nearly fifty acres.

By this time he had been given permission from the council to build a portable wooden structure to use as a shop to sell his produce. He soon found it necessary to purchase his fruit and vegetables from an outside source as he could not keep up with the demand from the customers. Every week he introduced new lines which included garden tools, furniture, seeds and bushes. He decided to extend his original greenhouse and purchased a new one with the manufacturers making the base and erecting the greenhouse. It would include central heating. Owen became an employer when he gave work to a teenager to help with the land cultivation and a young girl to serve in the shop. Both were full time. It was not long before he was back in the land purchasing a further twenty acres. The family wondered why he wanted so much land, as it was not likely he needed more than the ten acres for market gardening. Owen knew the family wondered but, like the rest, they would soon find out.

Over the next few years he cultivated over five acres and had to employ two part-time workers, as well as another full time man. Owen was able to assess his needs and predict the future development of the business and commercial prospects and he concluded his probable final purchase of land when twenty acres were offered to him. He then decided to build some houses on the original land he bought and engaged an architect to prepare outline drawings. Once he received planning permission the land was put up for sale. It was quickly sold and the sum paid to him was over twenty times what he paid for it. The quickness of the sale made him think that if land was worth as much as that then he should look into it as a secondary business.

Owen was a shrewd business man and even though he may not be liked or trusted it could not detract from the progress he had made in a short time. He asked Rhys to be manager of the gardening centre now it was established, but he had to decline because of his health. Owen was most disappointed as he knew he would be an asset to the business. When he looked closely at Rhys he realised how ill he looked and when he knew Rhys could see him looking at him he changed the subject. To accommodate the new manager he appointed, he bought the other half of the semi-detached he lived in.

Llewellyn mentioned to Owen some land for sale on a farm outside the village and asked him not to mention his name if he went to look at it as the farmer was a personal friend, and knowing how Owen tended to bully a seller into accepting as low a sale price as possible it would do nothing for the friendship.

Owen and the farmer eventually agreed on a sale price even though it was less than the asking price. The farmer asked Owen how he knew the land was for sale and without thinking gave him Llewellyn's name. It was a long time before the farmer spoke to Llewellyn after that.

Owen decided to buy a detached house outside of the village and it included some land with the sale. Jean was more than pleased as it gave her more privacy. The house had been neglected during and after the war, but again he decided to make his own repairs and redecorate, but he involved Jean, and it was a task she enjoyed doing. Once the house was ready they moved in and again she saw little of Owen as the business took up most of his time. She only appeared to see him at meal times and even then he was half asleep eating his evening meal.

Owen, for all his secretive nature and deviousness, realised how useful it was to discuss some of his business activities with Rhys and started to call on him on his way home from work and would ask him out for a drink. Their conversation was of a general nature and Rhys felt he wanted to know more about the family and in particular about the four brothers in the Second World War.

He continued to be successful with his business ventures and always seemed to be buying land and started to lease or rent to manufacturers and commercial concerns. His home and personal life with Jean were never satisfactory. It was no fault of Jean as she tried hard to make him a good wife. He never had to wait for meals and the house was always spotlessly clean. Their child was a credit to them both. Jean kept herself attractive for him, though not knowing what time he would be home made life difficult.

Owen and Jean attended family weddings and both enjoyed themselves and it was almost like when they were first married, but in the end pressure of work meant he did not see the family as often as he would have liked to and by the time the past caught up with him Rhys and John had died. Owen tried hard to pull back the time to make up for the years already gone and did partly succeed and became more of a brother.

OWEN SAID TO LLEWELLYN,

'I promised not to say you gave it to me.'

THE PARADE

As the hymn finished and the band stopped playing the RSM moved forward after having a brief conversation with the Officer commanding the parade.

The RSM shouted,

'PARADE, PARADE SHUN'.

As one they responded to his command and he could be heard saying, 'Well done.' The OC said to the parade, 'We will sing the National Anthem.' With everyone standing to attention the band started to play with everyone joining in.

Mae hen wlad fy'n hadau yn annwyl i mi,
Gwlad baedd a chantorion en wogion o fri,
Ei gwrol ryfelwyr gwlad garwyr tra mad,
Dros ryddid gollasant eu gwaed,
Gwlad, gwlad, pleiddeol wyf i'm gwlad,
Tra mor yn fur, i'r bur hoff bau,
O bydded i'r heniath bar hau.

As the last two lines were repeated Llewellyn's thoughts went back to Jean who found it necessary because of the lack of love from Owen to seek affection from others.

JEAN SAID TO LLEWELLYN,

'I hope Owen remembers he has a wife before it is too late.'

JEAN SAID TO LLEWELLYN,

'I hope Owen remembers he has a wife before it is too late.'

JEAN. Llewellyn thought she had a lot more character than most of the family gave her credit for, and certainly more than Owen. Her manner to most people was brusque and unfeeling but there seemed to be no reason for this and perhaps it was only her manner. She also tended to be shy and lacking in self-confidence. This again could be attributed to Owen as he never considered anyone and his business exuberance made others develop a lack of any form of confidence. With Jean it made no difference how long one knew her as she would be more than likely to treat one without any feeling, or make a fuss over one. It was better to be a little intrepid until one knew the mood she was in.

After her marriage to Owen and the necessity of being on her own for long periods she had no opportunity to know people. Owen loved her very much, but the need to establish his business had to take priority and home life became having meals and then to bed and within a few seconds off to sleep. He was naturally secretive and reticent in his dealings with others so Jean could expect no more from him and it should be remembered he could not always judge her moods.

Jean was a good violin player, and had a nice singing voice but without someone to listen to her playing there was no joy in it. What she lacked was visitors to her home, especially women friends to talk to, and not necessarily members of the family. It was difficult to bridge the gap she had created through having to spend most of her time on her own and having to stay near the telephone to answer business calls for

Owen. When she went shopping there was the odd occasion when she would talk to other shoppers, but if someone was too pushing she would back away. It was the same when Owen had a bad day at work and she would have to take the brunt of his frustrations.

It was seldom the family and friends were invited to the house as he was never there, and Jean would say to Llewellyn, 'I hope Owen remembers he has a wife before it is too late.' One could feel sorry for the both of them as they drifted apart in an indefinable manner with neither of them wanting or able to do anything about it.

Jean did her weekly shopping at the local supermarket on the same day every week. Her young daughter stayed with her mother, and she would usually collect her at 7 o'clock or Owen would pick her up on his way home from work. At the supermarket checkout, as it was lunch break for the staff, only the one was on duty, usually the older one who Jean knew because of her regular weekly visit, but they exchanged more than pleasantries when her groceries were checked.

This particular day when Jean handed over the money to the checker and one of the coins fell on the floor, and both of them without thinking went for the coin and in doing so their hands touched and neither said anything when their eyes met but both were transfixed and Jean felt her face reddening, and the checker seemed to feel the same. After that a special feeling developed between them. Jean would look forward to the weekly shopping, and both would look out for the other. If Jean was the only one at the checkout both would make an excuse to touch the other. This to others appeared to be casual, and without significance. Each week afterwards it was a wave when they saw each other, and they seemed to develop a form of visual lovemaking, and at the checkout their hands would tremble, and one of them would drop a coin and both their hands would go for it and in those few seconds they gripped each other tightly, and it became harder to appear casual in front of others.

When Jean went the following week to do her shopping the checker was not there and Jean was in a panic as she went around the shelves. She paid for her order and left quickly, and almost in a trance until she saw the checker waiting outside for her. They looked at each other as if the heavens had opened up especially for them. She said to Jean she had taken a half day off work. This was the first time they formally introduced themselves as Jean and Wendy. Jean asked if she would like to come home with her for a coffee, and nothing more was said until she opened the front door and let Wendy in first. Jean closed the door, and both went into the kitchen. Wendy watched as Jean put away the groceries, and as she made a cup of coffee for both of them.

On the surface both appeared to be happily married women, with husbands who loved them and were ambitious. Yet both of them could lose a lot if their liaison was found out, but they had the courage to see each other in spite of maybe losing everything. In their favour because they were able to keep their husbands contented, and decide it was worth all this rather than go back to the misery of their lives before they met.

Both accepted the relationship had long passed the point of no return and could only wait for the blast which would come. Owen may have wondered what brought the change in Jean, but could not be more pleased than at any time of their married life.

Jean and Wendy went on holidays together and both would take their child with them. It seemed the arrangements suited Owen as he could never find the time to take a holiday and he would often suggest to Jean she should go, but her reply was that she had no one to go with her. That was now all changed after asking Owen if she could go with Wendy. He raised no objection. It was the start of both of them regularly taking their holidays together with the two children, and with the blessing of both husbands and as Owen's business prospered so he had less time for anything other than business.

Jean and Wendy were the soul of discretion on all occasions, and both worked hard to ensure they did not damage their husbands' businesses, or lose the trust as far as their husbands were concerned. Jean was sure Owen knew more about her friendship with Wendy, but as the arrangements suited him he never questioned her and she never neglected him or their daughter. Owen was nobodys fool and thought it best to leave things well alone. Jean and Wendy met regularly and often talked about their present arrangements, still living in their husbands' homes. They decided if either husband started

100

making it difficult then they would both leave them, and set up a home for themselves and take the children with them.

JEAN SAID TO LLEWELLYN,

'I hope Owen remembers he has a wife before it is too late.'

THE PARADE

As the band started to play the anthem so those attending the parade braced themselves and started to sing,

'God save our gracious Queen.'

and concluded with the last line

'God save our Queen.'

When the singing stopped the Officer commanding the parade walked over to speak to the bandmaster and asked for the band to form up at the front of the parade and at the same time asked the standard bearers to follow behind them. As they were lining up Llewellyn's thoughts went back to his brothers and how when they all joined the Territorial Army all those years ago, Gareth who was only five feet tall took charge and marched them to the bus stop and said with a big smile, 'Well done.'

With Gareth's name on the wreath Llewellyn remembered his smile as though it was only yesterday.

GARETH SAID TO LLEWELLYN,

'Tell Llewellyn I will look after Glenys
until he comes home.'

GARETH SAID TO RHYS,

'Tell Llewellyn I will look after Glenys until he comes home.'

GARETH was the third oldest brother and at five feet tall the shortest. He joined the Territorial Army in the middle of 1939. If he had waited until after the start of the war he may not have been accepted because he was so short and also would not have had a choice of a regiment. There may be little of Gareth, but he would not let anyone bully or intimidate him and did not consider it necessary to ask his brothers for help. The knowledge that each of his brothers had gone through the growing up stage without help to fight their battles meant he had no option but to do the same.

Gareth was born in the twenties and from birth his mam said he was never any trouble and when people looked into his pram he would be smiling. At school he was in the beginning a slow learner and only by hard work was he able to keep up with the rest of the class, but was good at sport and played cricket and rugby for the school. Because he was short he became the butt of some of the teachers' frustrations, but never flinched or cried out when caned. It was a code of honour not to let them see they hurt him and would have a fixed smile. This would further provoke them to cane him all the harder. Over the school years it became a battle of wits between them, but they never had the satisfaction of knowing if they won because he gave no hint to accommodate them. When a teacher decided to send him to the headmaster to punish him he was less severe with him than the teacher would have expected, as the headmaster realised punishment was not the way to win the respect of Gareth. Over the years the relationship between them improved into an uneasy peace. The teacher did say some some years afterwards it was necessary to have a battle of wits with him or he would not have got the best out of him. Once they settled their differences Gareth started to enjoy learning.

Summer and winter he never liked going to bed and when his mam called him to say it was time for bed and his reply was, 'I'll be there in a minute', he never went in and there would be another call from his mam and his reply would be, 'I am already coming in' but still Gareth never went in and at this stage would have to decide whether to chance another call from his mam. This was a nightly battle between them, but he knew he could not win against her and would be reminded with a wallop. Llewellyn would say to him he should now learn from all this, but to Gareth it was a question of judgement and then accept the consequences when proven wrong.

All the time Gareth was developing natural leadership qualities, mostly by example. He seldom played with his brothers and if he did it was usually with Rhys, but he was at least nine inches taller than him and as the older Gareth would take charge. Gareth was good at cricket and rugby and was in the first team at school. The sports master thought he had potential as a left-hand spin bowler and gave him extra coaching. Gareth was made captain for his last year at school. He was not able when playing rugby to have it all his own way and he received as good as he got, and this was respected by others on the field. Gareth may have thought on many occasions the referee had not seen an incident he committed, but he would seek out Gareth and wag his finger at him.

The stubborness which was a natural trait in his character which many had tried to change eventually cost him his life as the Colonel of his regiment said in his letter to his mam when the same stubborn streak made him the target of the German soldiers on the Arromanches beach during the Normandy landings, when it could have been as easy to have found a more protective coverage, but the cost of lives of the other members of the regiment would have been greater. Gareth was awarded a posthumous Mention In Dispatches for his action.

Gareth's rigid code to accept the same standards as his brothers gave him a sense of pride whenever they went out together. Mostly he was dad's boy, and the family knew that, but occasionally he would overstep the mark and it would end up either with fighting or a battle of words and as he would not give up there was no satisfaction. Gareth learned the hard way with rugby that he could not take on the bigger boys and expect to win every time and however hard he tried his body was too small to absorb the punishment handed out to him. Eventually he found out they neither liked a dummy pass, nor a side step against them, so he was finding out one did not have to prove physically one was their equal to beat them.

When Gareth left school his dad was able to get him accepted as an apprentice electrician at a local electrical contracting firm. They specialised in house wiring and repair work and taking on sub-contract work. He was able to come in contact with more people and he enjoyed working with his hands. He went to night school to obtain a City and Guild certificate.

Gareth found it difficult involving himself with girls because he was too short, but his employer had a daughter called Ann who was five feet seven inches tall and he avoided her if possible.

His mam was more than pleased he was learning a trade and he completely rewired their house and included power points and installed a new electric cooker his dad bought. It certainly made life easier for his mam.

It was a long time before he had a conversation with Ann and it came about when his employer asked Gareth to pick up some equipment he had left at home. When he knocked at the door Ann answered and after a few difficult moments gleaned what he wanted. After that occasion she always spoke to him when she worked in the office. Once he started to know her he asked for a date. Ann could hardly say yes quickly enough. They enjoyed each other's company even though she was a lot taller. She on occasions wore low heeled shoes to make her look smaller, but he took exception and said she should wear her high heeled shoes. She never said anything to Gareth, but it made her proud of him. They would meet a few times in the evenings and on Saturday night. They enjoyed walking and holding hands and silly things like looking at each other. To them it was a form of love-making which was sufficient for them to know they were falling deeply in love with each other.

When he decided to join the TA before the war started it was to ensure he had a choice of regiments and probably be accepted as he was short. However, Rhys went with him to the drill hall the night he joined and afterwards he asked Rhys what he said to the medical corporal before he was medically examined, but he would not say. (His medical records stated he was five feet five inches tall. He was sworn in and given the 'King's Shilling' and no mention was made about his height and his medical records were never changed).

Gareth and Rhys were in different regiments, but went on the same night for TA drill and a pint in the mess afterwards. He enjoyed the discipline of the army. Ann saw less of him but was pleased he was with his brothers.

Gareth's employer was pleased with his daughter's choice and hoped it would lead to them eventually getting married. They both talked about marriage and left the date for another time. He wanted his apprenticeship completed first, but in the end even that was not completed.

The brothers' big event was the annual TA camp and the four shared two dates for going to camp, with Llewellyn off to Tidworth, Gareth to North Wales. John and Rhys went down to the south of england. (John and Rhys never came back from TA camp as they were mobilised during the two weeks and Llewellyn never saw them again until 1946.)

Gareth and Ann were giving serious thought to getting married and they decided to leave it for another year. Gareth was called up on Friday 1 September 1939. He was only stationed sixty miles away and they were able to see each other regularly. Both dreaded leaving each other on the Sunday night. They never wanted other company and neither made a move to satisfy the deep yearning which was always present, not because they never had the opportunity but even when they reached the heavy petting stage, would pull apart.

After six months his regiment moved to the south-east of England when the fall of France became a reality in May 1940. There was the possibility of an invasion by the German Army.

Llewellyn was posted overseas, with John following shortly afterwards. Gareth and Rhys always looked up Glenys when they were on leave and when Rhys was posted overseas Gareth said to Rhys, 'I will look after Glenys for Llewellyn.'

Gareth and Ann again thought about getting married, but

again decided to leave it for another year. (They could never make their minds up.)

He had the opportunity to join the Royal Engineers, but said he wanted to stay with a fighting regiment. His regiment spent about three years training for overseas duty, but at the last minute their orders were changed. By this time there were rumours of the second front.

Gareth was sent on embarkation leave in May 1944 for seven days. It was over four years since he was called up and at last knew something big was coming off and he wanted to be part of it. He told Ann the training they had would now be put to good use.

Ann knew it was going to be dangerous for him and again they talked about getting married, but as usual never made the decision, or even a date other than to say it would more than probably be on the next leave. They spent most of the leave together and both families left them on their own. On the Thursday it was decided they should go away until the Sunday night. It was Ann's dad who made the suggestion and he gave Gareth an envelope with the train fare to Tenby with the cost of the hotel and spending money. At first he did not want to take the money, but her dad told Gareth he could pay him back after the end of the war. They left in time to arrive at the hotel in time for lunch, and booked in as husband and wife, but it was obvious to the other guests they did not even look married.

Throughout the holiday they never spoke to anyone unless it was in answer to others. They were on time for meals, and would whisper to each other 'I love you'. They returned home on the Sunday evening, but again the families left them on their own. Ann saw Gareth off from Neath railway station on Monday afternoon and she broke down in his arms as they said goodbye. Ann had a letter from him and he said how much he enjoyed the holiday together and how he wished they had married many years before. He also mentioned that the regiment were making final arrangements to ship out.

The regiment moved the next day and travelled all night and stayed on the train most of the following day. Hot meals were prepared for them. In the evening they embarked on the ship and thought it was either Portsmouth, or Weymouth. They spent the next few days listening to lectures by their officers or playing cards. They had no communication from the ship. In the early hours of Wednesday evening the ship raised anchor and sailed for France. The regiment transferred to the landing craft with B company late on Thursday 7 June and were ferried to the Arromanches beach during the Normandy landing. Gareth waded ashore from the landing craft and within the hour he was killed.

GARETH SAID TO RHYS,

'Tell Llewellyn I will look after Glenys until he comes home.'

THE PARADE

The RSM walked to the front of the parade, and spoke to the bandmaster, and then returned to the Cenotaph and stood with the Officer commanding the parade.

The parade in column of route

Parade parade shun

Parade parade right turn

Parade by the left quick march

As the command finished the officer moved quickly to the front of the parade. The band as it moved off played 'Semper Fidelis' by Sousa. The parade marched through the town to the appreciation of the people who lined the pavements.

As Llewellyn marched with the parade his thoughts went back to when he first saw Ann with a young child who was the image of Gareth, but with the same colour hair as Ann. It was LLewellyn's first time home since he was demobbed and when he spoke to her she burst into tears and their thoughts went back to Gareth. Llewellyn held her hand for a moment and looking at her he said, 'Gareth would have been proud of you,' and with his eyes filling up said 'you had a first amongst men,' and looking down at her son said, 'you now have another first.'

ANN SAID TO LLEWELLYN,

*'We never could make our minds up
when to get married.'*

109

ANN SAID TO LLEWELLYN,

'We never could make our minds up when to get married.'

ANN. She first saw Gareth when he was at school and she remembered he played cricket and rugby for the school. She often wondered when he would start to grow taller because he was so much shorter than her, but there was something about him which made her think of him on more than the odd occasion, especially as she had little interest in the other local boys. Ann saw him next when she walked into the workshop of her dad's electrical firm and Gareth was standing at the work bench. He appeared not to notice her. When Ann spent longer periods on the premises keeping the paperwork filed properly she would always say good morning to him and when he answered her it was his longest conversation with her, but he would never stop work.

The first real opportunity came when he was sent to her home for some special tools her father had forgotten to take when he left for work in the morning. Gareth knocked at the door and she was most surprised to see him. He told her what he wanted and when she gave them to him he turned to go, but suddenly stopped and asked if she would like to go out with him. Ann said yes almost before he finished asking her. Later they disagreed about when their first date was. They had a very interrupted courtship because of his night school and TA training. Ann fell deeply in love with him and even though she had opportunities to go out with other boys it was always Gareth she wanted.

Ann's parents were pleased when she brought him home for a Sunday tea, and to watch them together required little imagination to realise how much they loved each other. She worried when he joined the TA like his brothers, but as Rhys would say to her he would never be killed with a bullet because he was too short. They all laughed. Ann felt a shiver run down her back and made her realise he was as vulnerable as the other brothers and she had good reason to remember this many years later.

Ann liked nothing better than going for long walks with Gareth. They would hold hands and never stop talking to each other. Perhaps they seemed an odd couple with Ann seven inches taller than him, but to her he was taller in ways that mattered, such as the ability to play rugby against bigger players, irrespective of how many times they put the boot in.

Neither thought to take their kissing beyond holding themselves tightly together.

Ann said the need to have sex never came into their conversation and they considered marriage the first priority, but making a firm date to get married seemed impossible and it resulted in a long courtship. Ann often said to Llewellyn we never could make up our minds when to get married. Before either of them knew it Gareth was on embarkation leave for overseas service and both of them thought it was France.

During the war years they were never able to have long periods together, usually limited to week-end and seven day passes, but they wrote regularly and his letters were neatly put away in bundles and marked with the year and Gareth would send her a parcel of her letters to him or bring them home on leave with him. Ann worried when he told her his regiment were given special training and there never seemed to be an end to the training over the last four years.

She met the train at Neath railway station and when he alighted from the carriage there was a new bounce about him. At the beginning of the leave they saw the relatives, but more and more only wanted their own company. Ann's dad suggested they take a short holiday so they could be on their own. Both thought it was a good idea and decided to go the next day and come back on the Sunday evening. Gareth called for her on the Thursday morning and just before they left her dad gave Gareth £30 and Gareth said he already had £20 from his dad. Her dad said he would need it all and when he thanked him her dad said to look after Ann and try not to delay things any longer. They left for Tenby by train and Gareth thought about Ann's dad and the conversation they had and wondered if he was talking about them getting married or, as his face started to go red, if it was what he was thinking about.

On the Friday evening after dinner Gareth proposed to Ann and she accepted. The next morning they went to the jewellery shop and asked to see some engagement rings. It took some time before she made her selection. She then knew why Gareth wanted to go to the post office with his savings book. She started to leave when he said they had not finished yet and with that Gareth said something to the owner of the shop. He went into another room and brought out a tray of wedding rings and as he showed them to her she burst into tears. The jeweller gave her a chair to sit on and fetched her a glass of water. When she recovered, with the help of the jeweller they picked the wedding ring she wanted. Gareth moved aside to pay and at the same time Ann could hear Gareth saying they would be ready today. As they walked out of the shop the jeweller took Ann to a large display cabinet and asked her to pick something of her choice. It would be a wedding present from him. It was a spontaneous gesture from him and for many years afterwards he wondered about the two of them who were very much in love, but at the same time there was something sad and he could only think of a present to them to remove his worry about them.

Gareth asked Ann to wait outside for him. She was puzzled by this. When she left Gareth asked the jeweller if he would engrave both rings and he wrote down what he wanted, and as he handed over the note asked if he could call later in the day. This was agreed, and Gareth paid for the rings and engraving and thanked the jeweller for the present he gave Ann. Ann intended asking him something when he came out of the shop, but looking at his face she said nothing.

They returned to the hotel for lunch, and Gareth saw the manager and asked if he could put on a special dinner for them. He found it difficult explaining the reason for an engagement dinner when they had already signed the register as married, but to Gareth a faint heart was no excuse for not telling the truth and the manager was pleased Gareth had confided in him and said he would make the arrangements. When they returned to the bedroom after lunch she asked what that was all about and all he would do was to ask her to dress up for dinner. They both slept for a few hours and Gareth dressed and went to collect the rings from the jewellery shop and called into the hotel on the way back for a bottle of champagne. The barman said it was expensive because it was in short supply, but Gareth was not interested in the price and took in upstairs with two glasses.

Ann looked up as he returned to the bedroom and after removing his battledress jacket sat down on the side of the bed and kissed her and said, 'I love you,' and then gave her the engagement ring she had chosen that morning. She tried it on and then removed it and read the engraving on the inside of the ring which said, 'Ann from Gareth 13/5/1944'. The misgivings of the morning and the missed opportunities of the years gone by evaporated and Gareth opened the champagne bottle and poured out two glasses and they drank a toast to themselves and then another glass each to drink to the families and almost finished the bottle. Ann then said to Gareth 'The longer I know you the more I love you,' and then, Gareth said to Ann, 'I will love you to the day I die.'

When they arrived at the dining table it was laid out with flowers and an engagement card from the management. Other guests offered them their best wishes and after a wonderful dinner they were given drinks by the other guests and eventually they joined them. When the engagement dinner finally broke up, and they went to their bedroom Gareth gave Ann the wedding ring he had engraved the same time as the engagement ring and told her to make the arrangements for their wedding on his next leave. Ann showed no emotion until she read the inside of the ring which simply said AIUIWWFYG1944 and even though she could not understand it the tears were building up. He gave her a letter which explained the meaning of the letters in the wedding ring saying that it would be better to read it after he had returned to camp.

They caught the train home and neither had much to say. Ann would look at her engagement ring and kept repeating the letters on the wedding ring and looking at Gareth hoping he would tell her and they were soon back to their usual talkative selves and in spite of a full carriage held hands with the occasional squeeze of hands.

113

Both families were waiting for them and everybody wanted to ask questions, but again held back so they could at least have the remainder of the holidays together. After giving his mam and dad a present they went to Ann's house and gave both her parents a present and sat down to lunch with them. Afterwards Gareth said he wanted to see his mam and dad and as he walked home realised it was the first time he was on his own since his leave started and felt so out of sorts that he wanted to have her by his side. Both his mam and dad could see this leave and the short holiday had a marked effect on Gareth and decided to let him do the talking. He told them Ann had agreed a date for their marriage on the likely assumption it would be a Xmas leave and that he had left the arrangements to her. They realised he knew full well that with the start of the invasion of France no date could be set.

The three of them sat down to a lunch with their heads full of questions to which there were no answers, but to his mam having him sitting at home was as much as she wanted. Shortly afterwards Ann came in and together they related the short holiday and showed them her engagement ring. The four of them sat all afternoon talking about the future, but mainly of the past. Ann then told Gareth her mam and dad were going out for the night and they suggested Ann made a meal for Gareth.

They returned to her home about five, and Ann started to make a meal for them and Gareth decided to help, and they were back to both talking at the same time and laughing at the least funny thing said. During the meal he asked if she had read the letter and she said she would read it tomorrow after he left. Both made the effort to enjoy themselves and not to think about the next day.

The remainder of the evening neither had much to say. They held hands and it was sufficient to hold each other until he looked at the clock and their thoughts were on returning to camp. It added a feeling of desperation and their kissing took on a new meaning and it was if the need for the other became urgent, and for the next few hours they made love in her parents front room with a passion so strong and purposeful it blotted out everything until Ann heard her mam shout to say she was home.

When they went into the living room Gareth caught the look

114

her dad gave her mam, then they looked at Ann and it was as if they shared a secret. Her dad went over to Ann and as he kissed her whispered 'Are you happy?' and she held him for a brief second.

A little over six weeks after Gareth returned from his leave his mam and dad went over to give Ann the telegram they received to say Gareth was 'Missing believed dead'. Ann could not be consoled with words. Everybody was careful what they said to her and all hoped the telegram would not be confirmed. The next few months were all the more difficult for Ann as there were no letters to write and the last letter she had from Gareth was shortly after he returned from his leave and all he was allowed to say were a few words to say they were on the move.

One evening a month later Ann told her mam and dad she was carrying Gareth's baby and the three of them were crying either for Gareth and then the joy of something positive to remember him by. She then went over to tell Gareth's mam and dad who were so pleased at the thought of a new baby to cushion the loss of her son. Shortly afterwards Gareth's mam gave Ann a letter she received that morning saying she had not opened it and thought the letter should be for her. Ann then asked if she could read the letter later on her own and his mam nodded.

Ann sat in her room and opened the letter. It was from the colonel of Gareth's regiment expressing his sorrow and sympathy with the family. He continued the letter by saying in the four years he had known him he was a first-class soldier, loyal, trustworthy and that he, the Colonel, would trust his life with Gareth. He said in the short period the regiment was on the Arromanches beach at Normandy Gareth fought with courage and complete disregard for his own safety when he drew the enemy machine-gun fire to himself for those few seconds so the others could proceed up the beach.

The letter was confirmation that she would not see Gareth in this life. She started to cry with the tears covering her face and her body shaking with the finalisation of her loss. Her mam and dad knocked on her door and went in to console her. She showed them the letter and said she hoped the baby would be a boy.

When her mam and dad left her she went to her box of

letters and removed the letter Gareth had given her on the last
night at the hotel when he gave her the wedding ring and
opening the letter she read that the letters AIUIWWFYG
meant 'Ann if unable I will wait for you Gareth'. She placed
the wedding ring on her finger and realising what he said was
that it would only be death which would stop him from marrying her on his next leave and that he would then wait for her.
She knew even before reading the words that there would
never be anyone else.

Many years later Ann asked Llewellyn and Glenys to take
her to see Gareth's grave and asked Llewellyn to make the
travelling arrangements. They left by car for Dover and then
across to Calais and on to St Valery en Caux where they stayed
the night at a local hotel. The next day they continued the
journey down the Normandy coast and stopped at Honfleur
for lunch and then on to the war graves' cemetery near the
outskirts of Bayeux.

Llewellyn told them to stay in the car until he checked the
graves' register, and then beckoned them on. Ann could see
the rows of headstones and the overwhelming atmosphere
started to take hold of her as she followed Llewellyn, and as
they neared Gareth's headstone they stopped and pointed out
the grave. They waited as Ann walked on and read the name
Gareth Edwards. She lost control of her feelings and
emotions. Glenys rushed forward and held her hands to try
and stop her shaking. They moved back when she regained
her composure. As they watched it seemed as though Ann was
talking to Gareth and telling him what a fine son he had and
that she would bring him with her next time she came.

After taking photographs they walked around the rest of the
cemetery and then Ann said a final goodbye to Gareth and
drove on to Arromanches. When they arrived Llewellyn asked
Ann if she would rather stay in the car, but she shook her
head. The three of them walked on to the actual area where
Gareth was killed. By then Ann had regained her composure
and looked at Llewellyn and Glenys and they could see how
proud of Gareth she was.

During the drive back to the hotel and after seeing his
headstone and where he was killed Ann felt more settled in
herself and at peace for the first time since he was killed and
that gave her the courage to keep going. At the same time it

116

brought back all her love for him and she knew Gareth would be waiting for her. The bunch of flowers she brought from her dad's garden had drooped by the time she placed them against the headstone, but as they came from Wales he would not mind.

Whenever she felt near to him she would remove his medals from the box in which she kept them and polish them until she had calmed down.

ANN SAID TO LLEWELLYN,

'We never could make up our minds
when to get married.'

THE PARADE

As the parade marched around the town the platform to be used as the saluting base was moved to the front of the Cenotaph, and the Lord Lieutenant with the Mayor and his party stepped on the platform to take the salute. The parade was fully appreciated by those lined up on the pavements. There was sufficient breeze to make the standards furl in the wind, and one could hear the chink of medals as the ex-service personnel marched behind the band and Standard Bearers. When the band drew up to the saluting platform they positioned themselves at the side, and the music changed to 'Old Comrades' by Teike.

When the first contingent reached the saluting base the order shouted was:

'PARADE. PARADE EYES RIGHT'

and this order was repeated as each contingent reached the saluting base.

As Llewellyn's head turned right his thoughts went back to John his eldest brother.

JOHN SAID TO LLEWELLYN,

*'A tramp walked into the saloon bar
and vomited on the floor.'*

118

JOHN SAID TO LLEWELLYN,

'A tramp walked into the saloon bar and vomited on the floor.'

JOHN was the eldest son and born before the end of the First World War, but his dad who served in France had not been able to marry his mam because he was made a prisoner of war in Germany in 1917. John never saw his dad until January 1919 when he returned from Germany. He had more love from his mam and family as a baby and was brought up only by the women in the family and this tended to make him selfish and jealous if more attention was given to others. When growing up he lost some of these traits. One feature noticeable was that he would lie easily and seemed to prefer it to the truth and after the attention he received as a baby he was not able to accept having to fend for himself when the other children were born. It isolated him from the family and he became more difficult to get on with.

John was one of the few persons who could say he attended the wedding of his mam and dad. He found being the eldest had the heaviest jobs to do around the house and would have the task of looking after the younger children when his mam had to work after his dad had an accident which kept him away from work for four years. John proved to be very capable and a lot of help to his mam.

When he was fourteen he started work as a miner's assistant at a colliery about six miles from home. He enjoyed working underground and soon had a reputation for being a hard worker. His weekly pay was 13/6 (67½p) and his travelling expenses were 2/6 (12½p). The coal-face he worked on was anthracite. He never mixed with other people and tended to be greedy and never satisfied until he had eaten too much and was too full to move. He was careful with his clothes and when

119

they became too small for him they would still be as good as new. His one bad feature was he thought that a lie was better than the truth and it never appeared to worry him.

His favourite subjects at school were geography and history and from an early age knew the name of most countries, where they were, their capital cities, and the currency. Dates of events were quoted in a flash.

Girls did not figure in his social life. It was not through want of trying but simply the fact they would go out with him a few times and then drop him. As one of them said 'He expects me to pay half shares.'

When Llewellyn and Rhys started work at the same colliery they would cycle to work and he would go by coach and would always be waiting for them with a cup of tea at the colliery canteen.

It seemed a pity John was never able to express his true feelings or able to communicate as he was a far better person than given credit for.

He joined the Territorial Army first and was a smart looking soldier and his mam and dad would watch him walking down the street in uniform until he was out of sight. John received promotion quickly which helped with his problem with other people, and in spite of some initial resistance he was winning over the men.

If it suited him he would revert to his old self. One particular occasion was a Saturday night out when the brothers finished in the local for a few drinks and when Llewellyn and Rhys went into the next bar for the drinks John waited in the saloon bar and when they returned there was vomit all over the floor and John's face was as white as a ghost. He looked the brothers straight in the face and said a tramp had walked into the saloon bar and was sick on the floor. They took him home and after undressing him put him to bed and he was asleep before they closed the bedroom door.

With all the talk of the pending war with the Germans the other three brothers joined the TA. During the months of July and August they went to annual TA camp.

When called up in 1939 John quickly settled down to army life and was promoted to sergeant and it was as if it was what he had always been waiting for. He would think to himself that he wished he had the leadership qualities of Rhys. John had a very hard war and was overseas until 1944 and served on the staff of the Divisional General where he specialised in signal duties. On his demob in 1946 he did not return to the colliery and found employment on the buses. He looked ill and had certainly aged and he had become more caring for other people. To supplement his wages he acted as a bookie's runner, but found it too demanding with his job on the buses.

John became restless and applied to emigrate to Australia. Before going he was invited to a regimental dinner in Scotland near where his general lived and during the visit met a young girl who lived in the village near to his hotel and eventually fell in love with her and she with him. John spent a few holidays at her village before he left for Australia and they agreed that when he settled down he would send for her. Catherine was a beautiful looking girl and was confirmed when she visited John's mam and dad.

Llewellyn travelled down to Southampton with John and went on board the ship. It was an emotional and sad goodbye. Llewellyn stayed on the docks until the ship was out of sight.

What John was looking for was respect and comradeship from others but he never realised other people judge one by how one behaves to them as much as they to one. John was beginning to accept this and making his own contribution to changing his ways.

Catherine and John were married within a week of her landing in Australia. They sent photographs of the wedding and the bungalow they were going to live at. John mentioned there were 300 acres of land with it, but had not made his mind up how much of the land he would cultivate as he was employed as a full time postman. John tried hard to make a good life for Catherine and she appreciated this and how nothing was too much trouble as far as she was concerned. All the time their love for each other was growing. Catherine knew John had not fully recovered his health from his war service and would watch for signs to alert her and at the same time not make it too obvious, and all the time would take some of the work load from him. Within a few years they had two children and nothing could please them more and even with the extra work they were starting to enjoy the Australian way of life.

John in his employment as a postman had a big round with

small holdings, sheep stations, farms, bungalows and small groups almost like a Welsh village. He was provided with a vehicle to make deliveries. He even passed on messages to neighbours and would pick up groceries to the more outlandish places. It was probably unofficial work but John enjoyed it and he became a popular visitor when he made his rounds. He would have liked to spend more time on the land, but with the post office duties and having little farming experience he could only make slow progress, and then he would have to ask questions of the other farmers and thought he was imposing on their generous nature. He did start by growing vegetables and building up his livetock, mainly beef for local slaughtering. Each year he would increase the market gardening and beef production and he employed some part-time labour. He did not want to give up his post office job as it gave him a regular wage packet and the money helped to fund the farm.

John and the family made a visit home to Scotland for Catherine and to Wales for him. The post office allowed him to accumulate his annual holidays over a period of two years. During their stay John spent most of his time in Wales and Catherine and the children came down from Scotland for the last week of their holiday. Towards the end of their stay John did not look well. They returned to Australia after five weeks. Both families would have liked them to have stayed longer but, as John said, it was expensive having to employ someone on the farm when they were away.

Some weeks after they returned to Australia John asked Catherine why she seemed so unhappy and she told him she was homesick for her parents and Scotland. Many years before he had promised her that if ever she wanted to return home there would be no argument from him. So they started making arrangements to put the farm and bungalow up for sale. Both worked hard to make the property an attractive sale and gave it to an agent to sell. Within a month it was sold for the asking price and they agreed with the purchaser to vacate in four weeks' time. When the agreement was signed, taking into account all the expenses, including the air fare and the transport by sea of those items they wished to take with them, there would be sufficient left over to buy a house and a small business in Scotland.

They were kept busy over the next few weeks arranging everything, packing the things being sent by sea. They completed everything and had nearly two weeks to enjoy a well earned rest. They decided to let the children remain in school until the last few days.

The new purchaser started to take over the farm work which left John and Catherine with nothing to do. John would take the children to school in the morning and Catherine had an extra lie in bed, and for the first time in many years they were able to concentrate on themselves without the worry of the farm. During the last week John complained to Catherine that he was not well. She went with him to the doctor who suggested he went for a check-up at the local hospital and stayed overnight. Catherine explained to the doctor that they were leaving for Scotland in a week, but the doctor said it would be better if John was to stay until the check-up was completed. John suggested returning to the bungalow, but she said it was for the best, so he agreed to stay. John died the next day.

JOHN SAID TO LLEWELLYN,

*'A tramp walked into the saloon bar
and vomited on the floor.'*

THE PARADE

As they marked time on the parade ground waiting for the rest of the parade to arrive so the Officer commanding the parade moved to the centre so that everyone could see him and, looking around, was satisfied with the turn-out. As the parade closed ranks he could distinctly hear the chink of medals.

In a loud voice he shouted:

Parade-parade halt

Parade-parade left turn

and the final command for the Remembrance Sunday parade,

Parade-parade dismiss.

The parade ground seemed a mass of people hurrying on their different ways, some to meet their wives and others old comrades, and the younger elements to their parents. Amid this activity Llewellyn remembered Catherine who was the only 'foreigner' in the family and John having to go all the way to Scotland to find her and saying to John that there is a girl for every one and that it is just a question of finding her. Llewellyn wished he could remember when he said that to John.

JOHN SAID TO LLEWELLYN,

*'I will send for Catherine
when I have settled in.'*

JOHN SAID TO LLEWELLYN,

'I will send for Catherine when I have settled in.'

CATHERINE was waiting for the bus to take her into town when someone asked her which bus to catch for the town. She said the next one due. When the bus came he had no option but to sit next to her. She had another glance at him and saw a pale young man dressed in one of the new demob suits. She knew the suit as men in her village who returned from the war were dressed similarly. When John spoke to her on the bus she had difficulty in understanding his accent and John said under his breath that it is not as funny as a Scots accent. They never said anything else during the journey to town and when the bus reached the town everyone got off. Catherine thought no more of him, but she did see him walking around the shops and he appeared to be lost.

In the early afternoon she went for a meal and looking around for a seat saw the stranger with the funny accent trying to attract her attention. She pretended not to notice and again looked for a vacant seat. He caught her eye and beckoned her over to his table. This time she could not avoid him and walked towards him and he pointed to an empty chair. She looked at his pale face and, thanking him, she sat down. John offered her the menu and said he was going to order and Catherine quickly gave her order as the waitress was waiting. As she took another look at the man at the table Catherine thought there was more to him than she first thought. She heard him saying his name was John Edwards and said she was Catherine. (Catherine said to Llewellyn many years afterwards that it was a strange first meeting with John and that she was so shy when he introduced himself that she was lost for words.)

125

Catherine thought how quickly the meal went by. He offered to pay for her meal, but she said no, but he did not seem to take any notice and paid for the both of them. Her next surprise was that they were walking together around the town. She told John it would be another hour before the bus left and wondered afterwards why she said that. Catherine was more than intrigued with him and wanted to ask what he was doing in Scotland, but did not want to rush this meeting. Returning in the bus to their village he told her he was staying at the local hotel and would be there for the next three days. He offered to walk her home from the bus stop, but she told him it was only a few hundred yards, but he took no notice and walked to her house and then asked if she would like to have a drink with him at the hotel later on. Catherine almost blurted out a yes and he said he would call for her at 7 o'clock.

When he knocked at her door at 7 o'clock a man answered who looked like her father. He invited John in to wait for Catherine and offered him a drink, but John thought better of it, as it was too early in the evening. Knowing how strong real whisky was he then asked if he could have a beer instead. He was introduced to her mother who then shouted to tell Catherine to say John had arrived. Her mother wondered why she showed so much interest in this young man.

Catherine thought to herself that John was very quiet as they walked to the hotel and wondered what his parents were like and started to read more into the date than she should, or was she? Both settled down in the lounge of the hotel and being a Saturday night it was busy, but neither even noticed the noise or anything else. Catherine listened while he told her about his 'old' general who had asked him to call after he returned from the regimental reunion dinner of his wartime staff.

As they walked towards her home when they left the hotel John searched out her hand and she kept asking herself what she was doing holding hands with someone who lived hundreds of miles away. She felt him squeezing her hand and all she could think of was to return the squeeze. When they arrived at her home she invited him in, but he said it was late. He looked at her as if he was going to kiss her, but instead asked if he could see her the next day. She suggested that as he was so far from home would he like to come to tea and with a quick yes he was gone. When Catherine went into her house her mam and dad were waiting. They looked at her face and then at each other, and thought to themselves that their only child was in love. During supper she could not stop talking about him and said she had invited him to tea tomorrow. It seemed to her as though the time could not go quickly enough for her to see him.

On Sunday afternoon Catherine was unable to concentrate on anything and kept looking at the clock. She tried to help her mam with the tea but in the end sat down with her dad. He held her hand and asked about John. She told her dad she knew little about him other than that he was in the army during the war and knew the General who lived on the outskirts of the village. When she heard the door bell ring she jumped up, but made her dad answer it. When her dad brought him in there was no sign of Catherine. In the end he had to call her from the bottom of the stairs to say John had arrived. She said a quiet hello to John when she came down and then promptly ignored him. Her dad smiled to himself and wondered what John would think if he had heard her extolling his praises earlier on.

Both her parents were successful during tea in breaking the shyness barrier and he told them about his mam and dad and the rest of his family. He mentioned there were four brothers in the army and that the second youngest had just completed his National Service. He started to tell them about Rhys and Gareth but felt his eyes filling up and asked to be excused. A few minutes later Catherine joined him in the sitting room and without thinking kissed him and to John it was the most wonderful thing in the world to have happened to him. He quickly recovered his composure and responded to her kiss by holding her tightly as though he was afraid of losing her. It was then they both realised they were in love. They went back into the dining room to finish their tea and they all started to talk at once and with that they all started to laugh. Her mam and dad were pleased at how well she coped with a sad situation. They went for a walk after tea, but both were quiet and did not want to break the other's reverie. They arranged to meet the next evening and John asked Catherine to thank her mam and dad for inviting him into their house. They stood by

127

her front door and as they kissed good night so they held each other tightly and John could feel her trembling.

When Catherine met him the next evening he asked if she would like to go to the pictures. Neither seemed to remember much about the film as they held hands and kissed each other until it was time to leave. On the way back to her home John told Catherine he was in love and she said she did not know falling in love could be so quick.

Her mam had supper ready for them and with the four of them at the table John told them about the time the four brothers joined the TA and how Rhys had to arrange with the medical corporal to add five inches to Gareth's height on his records to enable him to join. John related what a wonderful personality he had and how good he was at cricket and rugby and how although only five feet tall never backed away from a fight and then John said how much the family missed him. It was then Catherine and her mam and dad realised he was dead.

All of them listened as John said about him courting Ann for over five years and how they both kept putting off getting married and about Ann having a son eight months after Gareth was killed on the beach at Arromanches on the second day of the Normandy landing. Nobody said anything for a few seconds until Catherine's dad asked if John would like a glass of whisky. John looked at the very full glass and even though it was a strong drink it soon went down and immediately there was another one for him. When it was time to leave he asked her if she would like to go with him tomorrow to see the General to give his goodbye to him. It would mean taking a day off from work, but it would be worth it to see such a famous General.

Catherine was ready and waiting when John knocked on her door the next morning and both were looking forward to the visit. The General was expecting them and when John introduced Catherine to him he told her he had seen her many times in the village, and he asked how long she had known John and she replied, with her face blushing, three days. Then John told the General how he met her.

The General told Catherine John had been a sergeant on his personal staff from 1942. He showed her photographs of his war-time staff and with special reference to John asked if she knew he had an award for bravery. When they were leaving the General told Catherine to call any time she wanted to and not to forget he would like an invite. Again she started to blush when she realised what he meant. When they were walking back to the village she asked John why he didn't tell her about the award, and she asked herself what further surprises would she discover about the Edwards' family.

It had been their intention on the last night before he returned to Wales to invite Catherine and her parents to dinner at the hotel he was staying at, but they thought otherwise by arranging a dinner for him at their house. When he arrived at Catherine's house for the dinner her mam was putting the finishing touches to the table. Catherine was helping her mam and as she looked at her daughter she could not remember her being so interested in anyone. She was pleased because John was such a nice person. He was given a glass of the best whisky by her dad and as he sipped it he could feel it warming his inside and started to feel more relaxed. He was offered another whisky but knew that if he had another one it would make him too talkative.

It was a marvellous dinner and when it was finished Catherine and her mam cleared the table and washed up almost as quickly, so her mam and dad said they were going over to see their friends and would not be back until 11 o'clock and he did fill John's glass up with whisky before he left. Catherine and John sat on the settee. He closed his eyes and went straight to sleep and as she looked at his face the lines showed he was not a well man. He woke up after thirty minutes and apologised for sleeping, but she stopped him with a kiss.

They spent the evening kissing and talking and even though they were very worked up and it needed only a gesture from the other to take their love-making further, neither thought it necessary. When they heard the front door opening slowly and a call from her dad they had enough time to collect their thoughts. John thanked her parents for the lovely evening and all the hospitality shown him during his stay. They were both appreciative of his thanks. When he said goodbye to Catherine at the front door he asked if he could come up in a month's time and before he could finish asking she said yes. John left early the next morning for the train trip to Wales.

When John returned home he was not the same person who left four days before. He had to tell his mam and dad about Catherine. He made regular trips to Scotland and Catherine came down to see his family. He told her about going to Australia and it did floor her for a few minutes and she wondered what her mam and dad would say. John did say he had arranged to go there before he met her and if she would rather he did not go then he would not. It then occurred to her that he was proposing, and when she recovered from the shock of the proposal she said yes. They chose an engagement ring together at the town near her village. Her parents had hoped she would marry from their home with all the relatives there, but they put these thoughts aside and gave them both their unreserved blessing. John spoke to her parents on his own and told them he would look after their daughter all his life and if Catherine was unable to settle down in Australia then they would sell up and come back to Scotland.

On the last visit to see Catherine before he left for Australia he invited them both to dinner with him and Catherine at the hotel he first stayed at. He told the manager it was a special occasion, coupled with an engagement party. It was a wonderful meal with champagne and table wine. John gave Catherine the engagement ring and they were officially engaged. John left the following morning and a few days later sailed to Australia. To Catherine it was a long wait, but they wrote regularly to each other. He told her about his new job as a postman near the town of Coolgardia near Perth in Western Australia. She would study the map, but it looked such a small place it was difficult to find.

Nine months later he wrote and told her he had put a deposit on a bungalow with 300 acres of arable land and with his job as a postman he would be able to meet the repayments to the bank with sufficient money left over for their day-to-day requirements. He mentioned rearing livestock and developing market gardening, but he would wait to discuss it between themselves. Catherine left by cargo ship which had limited passenger facilities. It was an emotional parting from her parents and taking her 'bottom drawer' caused a few problems as it needed a few large boxes. The journey was slow, and long, with the ship calling at most of the major ports on its way to Australia, but it was an experience she would not have missed. John was waiting at the docks in Perth. She could wave to him but he was not allowed on board.

Eventually her luggage was removed and put into temporary storage at the docks warehouse. Driving into Perth from the docks neither could stop talking. John said he had booked some rooms at a small hotel and would leave the next day for their home. In the morning they returned to the docks for the large luggage. Eventually they were on their way. She looked at his face as they drove and thought it was leaner, with some colour. The van he hired was slow and it would probably mean sleeping in it for the one night but they kept stopping and reaching out for the other and holding the other tightly, repeating the pattern all the way home. It was a joyous occasion after such a long time. John asked lots of questions about both families. She would ask about the bungalow and the timed seemed to flow, and all the time both would express their love for the other. John arranged for her to stay with friends until the wedding on Saturday. She felt strange being so near to him, but still not with him.

They had a marvellous wedding day with all John's friends trying to make a special effort as Catherine's parents were not there. They decided not to have a honeymoon because she wanted to be in her own home.When they were on their own both felt strange being on their own for the first time as a married couple. Neither wanted to suggest it was time for bed, but in the end they just drifted to the bedroom. It took a long time for them to get to sleep, but they clung to each other as if they were the only people in the world. Cathering would try and look at his face as the morning came and could see that in spite of the healthy looking tan he was not well.

John woke up early on their first Sunday morning as a married couple, and made a cup of tea for them both and Catherine woke as he carried it it into the bedroom, and for the first time they both felt comfortable with each other. They both had a busy morning with Catherine preparing lunch and John feeding the few calves he had and the chickens. They were starving by lunch time and tucked in and enjoyed the meal. There was some wine left over from the wedding, which they drank, and some of the tension of the previous night was still there and as suddenly as the wrong word was said she burst into tears. It was almost uncontrollable. John half

131

carried her to the settee and they sat holding on to each other. She was trembling and her face was wet with tears and the more he tried to console her the more she cried. It lasted over an hour until she eventually stopped and the trembling eased off. John dried her eyes and for the first time since she landed in Australia they looked at each other properly and their true love for each other showed itself and the turmoil of the last few days evaporated. They slept for a few hours and Catherine woke up first and as John woke up he saw her looking at him and she asked if he would like a cup of tea.

From their first Sunday together neither looked back as they achieved the harmony of their physical expression of the love they both had for the other. They worked hard improving the bungalow and developing the land to include vegetables and flowers, with additional livestock. It took them five years to save enough money to take a holiday in Scotland. A short time before they made the final travel arrangements Catherine found she was pregnant so they delayed the holiday. In fact, it was many years before they made the journey to Scotland and by then there were two children. When they eventually made the trip her mam and her dad were overjoyed to see the children and her daughter, and looking at John, they knew she had made the right choice and they could see how much they were in love. Both of them and the children went down to Wales so they could see their other grandparents and stayed two weeks.

John's mam asked him how he was and had the usual all right from him. When they returned for the last few days they invited Rhys to go up with them. Catherine's mam and dad noticed the likeness between them although Rhys was taller. He thought Scotland was a marvellous country, and he enjoyed the whisky. John told Catherine's mam and dad that Rhys was a captain and had a very hard war. As they looked at him they could see that even though he was still a relatively young man, his face and stoop were the price he was paying for his war service. They also realised he was someone who would be a better friend than an enemy.

Catherine until then never had the opportunity to have a talk with Rhys but as hard as she tried he gave her few details, but she knew that, like the other brothers, there was a lot more to them and their mam and dad must have been proud of them. She felt he must have had to do some terrible things during his war service. Catherine said she was proud to now be a member of the Edwards' family.

Rhys returned home to Wales on the same day John and his family started their journey back to Australia. There was lots of crying and emotional upset and Catherine seemed more prone to shedding a tear. John put it down to being homesick for Scotland. When they returned the both of them worked hard with the development of the land and making a small profit from the sale of market gardening produce.

John continued to have bouts of ill health and Catherine would worry about him so she decided they would all go on a picnic on the next Sunday and have a relaxing day. They set out in the morning to the local beauty spot and Catherine made plenty of food for them all, with soft drinks for her and the children and beer for John. To work up an appetite they played games with the children and after the picnic the children went for a walk, and they had a little sleep. John woke up when he heard Catherine crying. He waited until she stopped crying and asked what was wrong. She said the holiday in Scotland had made her homesick to be back there. John told her that the promise he made a long time ago still stood.

On the Monday morning they made arrangements to sell the bungalow and land with the livestock and market gardening as a going concern. Catherine could not have been more pleased if he had given her the crown jewels. They had little difficulty in selling to one of their neighbours. It was agreed the sale would coincide with them leaving for Scotland, but the new owner would be responsible for the farm two weeks earlier which would leave them a free two weeks at the bungalow with the handover and exchange of contract five days before the flight from Perth.

On the Sunday of the start of the second week John felt ill and went into hospital for a check-up. The next day John died. There was not a time when Catherine felt so completely lost. The funeral was a nightmare and without their friends helping she would never have managed.

Catherine telephoned her parents and John's and told them what had happened. The thought of her and the children leaving Australia without John was upsetting and she went to see the local minister of the church they were married at. His advice was to go home, as agreed with John, who would be in Australia, the place he decided many years ago he wanted to be. Catherine made her final visit to the cemetery and talked to John as if he were standing beside her. She made her goodbyes as the tears ran down her face. She remembered John saying many years ago, 'Catherine I will love you all of my life.'

JOHN SAID TO LLEWELLYN,

'I will send for Catherine
when I have settled in.'

THE PARADE

The parade ground quickly thinned out when those on parade were dismissed and as Llewellyn saw Glenys and Sian walking towards them they looked cold. Llewellyn made his goodbyes with a handshake to his old comrades and friends. Walking towards the British Legion club he nearly stumbled and Glenys asked if he was all right and he said he had been dreaming, and she asked him what about, and he asked if she remembered the engagement party of Rhys and Gwen when she left in a hurry because Rhys had too many dances with one of the other girls there and she had chased after her and told him not to think he had upset her. 'Just refuse to let him see you thought anything about it.'

RHYS SAID TO LLEWELLYN,

'There could never be anyone like Gwen in the whole wide world.'

RHYS SAID TO LLEWELLYN,

'There could never be anyone like Gwen in the whole wide world.'

GWEN first saw Rhys when he came into the shop where she worked to buy a packet of cigarettes, but thought little about it until he looked around when leaving the shop and said to her 'So long for now.' She began to notice he had started to call in the evening for cigarettes as well as the morning, but never said more than his order and a 'So long' as he left the shop. (She would have been surprised if she knew he only smoked about five cigarettes a day and the shop was not on his way to work.) Some mornings and evenings, if Gwen was not working in the shop, her friend would say to her he was very disappointed she was not there to serve him. When Gwen realised the only reason he was calling at the shop was to see her she started to take notice of him and saw someone who was tall with a slight stoop, and not looking well. What she noticed more was a wonderful smile and eyes which compelled her to keep looking at him. Gwen had seen him in the village before he became one of her customers. Rhys told Llewellyn about Gwen and wanting to see her, but not knowing quite how to go about it. Llewellyn said nothing but thought it better to let things take their own course, as is with true love.

One evening when she was leaving the shop Gwen noticed Rhys waiting for her. She wondered if he had been waiting straight from work. She looked across at him and smiled. Rhys walked towards her pushing his bike and he returned her smile. She felt her body tingling and her face turning red. He asked if he could walk her home. Gwen said she had never met a person like him. He had a quality of happiness, but clouded by a secret of an unavoidable fate, coupled with a not easily

136

penetrable soul. Gwen shrugged off the feeling, but later was to be reminded of this. When Gwen said yes to Rhys they walked towards her home. When they arrived he introduced himself by saying, 'I am Rhys Edwards and I know your name.'

Rhys would say many times afterwards that meeting Gwen was the best thing ever to happen to him. This was understandable as she had the true Welsh features highlighted by her striking bone structure with dark brown eyes, thick browny-red hair and a Welsh temper. Rhys was the perfect antidote for her temper. Gwen and Rhys started to see each other regularly and would always be on the telephone to each other. It was remarkable the effect Gwen had on him as he felt like a lot of other ex-servicemen who missed the opportunities to spend their years as a youth with the family and friends of their own age or losing five or more years of their youth because of war service. When Gwen and Rhys had their engagement party he had too many dances with someone else and Gwen was so hurt she left the party and it was only the intervention of Glenys who saved the day. It taught Rhys a lesson in reminding him that those he loved should not be ignored.

In the meanwhile Jean and Owen were married and settled down. He would say his National Service in the Royal Air Force was good training for civvy street. Rhys and Gwen enjoyed their company and would make a foursome for a night out.

Gwen and Rhys spent their honeymoon at a local hotel for two nights and within twelve months their baby girl was born and soon afterwards a baby boy. Both were highly delighted with both children. They were quite contented with their own company and there was never a morning when she did not see him off to work and she would be waiting when he arrived home in the evening.

What or who would want to disturb such an ideal marriage where love was equally given as received and yet over the years and when the children were growing up Gwen noticed the health of Rhys was giving some concern, not necessarily noticeable to strangers, but Gwen knew every line on his face, and every additional white hair on his head. Gwen did say after the first ten years of marriage that Rhys began to tire very easily. They put it down to his war service in the far east, and the conditions they were fighting under and against the Japanese soldiers who never gave up, and also the humidity, rain, insects, lack of sleep, and the fear of never knowing when the enemy would attack them. Rhys never recovered fully from the bouts of malaria and dysentery which made life intolerable. He told Gwen it was no easier for the men than for the officers. Gwen suggested he saw a doctor and when he eventually agreed he was sent to a specialist.

Their love-making evaporated, and for a couple who were equally participating partners a coolness developed between them, until commonsense prevailed and they realised it was only themselves they were hurting and it was out of their hands until his health recovered. Both made attempts to adopt a less active form of love-making to satisfy their basic needs, but Rhys was not capable and both of them came to terms with it, and finally were content to express their love by holding each other and kissing. Even then he would be the first to relax his hold on Gwen and she could see he was exhausted. All this only drew attention to his illness and made him feel worse.

Rhys would tell Llewellyn there could never be anyone like Gwen in the whole wide world and their marriage was good for them in spite of his continued illness.

Rhys started to attend hospital more often for treatment and received all the support possible from Gwen. He did not like the idea of Gwen asking the Specialist what was wrong with him but at the same time told her that if it were serious he would tell her. The word 'treatment' brought on a fear that Rhys was not telling her everything, and what if it was not successful. She did realise he was to some extent trying to shield her until the end if it was worse than thought.

Glenys started to visit Rhys as she could remember how she looked after him when he returned home afte the war. Gwen knew there was a special relationship between Rhys and her. Gwen would not even ask Glenys what was wrong with Rhys as she felt honour-bound knowing he would not let her down if the illness was not cured. But with Rhys beginning to attend the hospital more frequently and for longer periods she did not need to be told but still tried not to make it obvious she was worried. Gwen dreaded the visits to the hospital as the fear he would want to tell her the obvious was becoming more of a reality.

As the bell rang to say the visiting time was over Rhys asked his mam and the rest of the visitors to wait in the corridor and motioned Gwen to stay. As they were leaving the ward the Sister put a screen around the bed. Gwen started to tremble when the Sister left and Rhys held her hands gently and she started to cry and he put his arms around her and held her face close to his and could feel her shuddering as she sobbed. Rhys wanted to calm her down and hold the wonderful creature for ever and ever and he told her what the specialists had told him earlier in the day and as Gwen went to speak he held his hand over her mouth and told her how lucky he was to have fallen in love with her and how thankful he was for the two children she brought into his life. He said that even though there was only a short time left the time they already had together more than made up for what was not to be.

The family returned to the ward to say cheerio and his mam kissed him with a special hug. Gwen said she would be back for the evening visiting, and silently said to him, 'Rhys, I love you and I love you.' Rhys died a few hours afterwards with Gwen sitting beside the bed holding his hands as she felt the last breath leaving him.

RHYS SAID TO LLEWELLYN,

'There could never be anyone like Gwen
in the whole wide wide world.'

THE PARADE

Phillip said to Llewellyn, 'You were in a funny mood this morning as each time I spoke to you there is no answer, and it is as though you are far away.'

Llewellyn said, 'It happens every Remembrance Sunday, and I find it difficult to adjust, especially belonging to a large family, and on the occasion that thoughts go back to how many of the family have gone.'

When Glenys and Sian arrived they asked if he was all right and Llewellyn said with a smile to prove it, 'I will let Phillip buy the first round in the club.'

RHYS SAID TO LLEWELLYN,

'Tell Mam there is no paper in here.'

RHYS SAID TO LLEWELLYN,

'Tell Mam there is no paper in here.'

RHYS was the fourth oldest son and decided from when he could remember that it was Llewellyn with whom he wanted to go around with and not Gareth. (It seemed Gareth always preferred his own company.) Until Llewellyn started his apprenticeship Rhys would never miss an occasion to go out with him and the rest of the gang, but if they decided not to allow him with them he would follow at a safe distance so if one of them ran back to catch him he would be far enough away not to be caught.

It seemed there was no time when Llewellyn could remember Rhys and him not being together as they went to school and came home together. Rhys was bright at school and always at the top of the class in exams. He was not keen on sport, but was handy with his fists and did not like to be beaten. He considered winning his fights important, but at the same time was not afraid of receiving a hiding. He gained a reputation for being a good fighter, and there was always someone wanting to take him on. As he grew older the other boys began to respect him and did little to provoke him. This could be seen as the period when the qualities of leadership developed.

Rhys loved his mam and dad. It was as if there was something special between the three of them. Yet he would stand up to his mam if he thought it necessary, but usually ended up the loser as she was tall and well-built, and the flat of her hand on the back of the head made Rhys think again but still chanced his arm, but after the second wallop discretion became the better part of valour.

The toilet or WC was stone built with a coalhouse attached

141

and both faced the back of the house. There was a path in between and used by the occupants of the houses further down and at each end of the terraced houses was a passageway and called a gully. Whenever Rhys went to the toilet there was no telling how long he would be in there and he would sing with the people in the other houses knowing it was Rhys in the toilet. No amount of shouting at him brought him out any sooner. The toilet paper was newspaper cut into squares and a length of string threaded through with a needle and hung on a nail. If there was no paper in there the whole street could hear Rhys shouting to Llewellyn to tell his mam there was no paper in there.

They were a large family when Owen, Andrew and Sian were born, but it was John who helped her around the house. One thing they all had was good appetites and on Saturday lunchtime they had, according to Rhys, the best meal of the week – bacon, tomatoes and fried bread. Their mam would buy bacon pieces at the Home and Colonial shop with a large tin of Crown tomatoes. Two loaves of bread would be cut and when they all sat down there was little talking and Rhys always kept back a piece of bacon and two slices of bread his mam had cut from the two loaves to make into a sandwich. He would finish by saying, 'A meal fit for a king.'

Rhys considered a pennyworth of chips for supper his second choice of a meal and would cut his chips in half longways and place them on a slice of bread and butter and top it with another slice of bread and butter. He would eat it slowly and enjoy every mouthful and would repeat the process until all the chips were finished. He certainly loved his chips. As Rhys would say, there was not much money coming into the house but their mam and dad made sure they always had plenty to eat.

When Rhys left school he became an apprentice fitter like his brother Llewellyn. They bought him a cycle to ride to work and he went the same time as Llewellyn. John went by coach. Now he was working and having pocket-money he would go with the rest of the gang to the town, and walk both ways, but he was too young to go into the pub, so it was fish and chips for him. He was popular at work with the men and fellow apprentice and could be trusted with any task given to him. Rhys had a natural smile with all he came into contact and he never resorted to backchat. The capacity for not looking for trouble was a lasting feature of the personality he was developing.

Rhys and John decided to join the Territorial Army together and shortly afterwards Gareth and Llewellyn joined up. It was always a mad rush on drill night to change into uniform and catch the bus into town and afterwards have a few drinks in the Naafi. The four brothers were not always able to have the same drill night because they were in different regiments. Whenever the four of them were out together they would pick Gareth to be acting NCO and give the command as though it was a drill night.

John was the first to receive promotion and as the oldest it seemed right and proper. The promotion suited him. Rhys certainly benefited from joining the TA. The officer commanding his regiment observed his latent leadership qualities and told his section officer to give him regular reports on his training progress. The highlight for them was two weeks' TA camp which involved training with the regular army at their depot, or under canvas. It was the only holiday which the employer was obliged by law to release them for the two weeks. They were paid the same as the regular soldiers.

In 1939 there were constant rumours of war breaking out in Europe. It was a source of worry to their mam and dad as the four sons would be called up at the same time if war were declared. Gareth and Llewellyn went on two weeks in July and returned from camp two weeks later, but John and Rhys were mobilised during their two weeks TA training and did not return to civvy street until 1946. Gareth and Llewellyn were called up 1 September 1939. Llewellyn was posted away and he did not see Rhys until 1946 and one brother he never saw again.

Rhys made rapid promotion strides and became a sergeant. It was a popular promotion as far as the officer commanding the regiment was concerned because it confirmed his original assessment of Rhys. The men in his section could not do enough for him. At rifle practice, unarmed combat or drilling on the parade ground his section were always amongst the top places. His ability to fight led him to boxing and eventually he became champion in his weight for the brigade. When Rhys was told by his mam she was considering informing the army that he was too young for military service at sixteen years of age he said to her he could not face going back to his apprenticeship, so she relented, but if she had known the consequences it may have been a different story.

On leave he spent time with Glenys and if Gareth was home the same time they would be a threesome. Both would say that someone should look after Glenys with Llewellyn away. When he went to the far east it only left Gareth, as John had been posted overseas some months previously.

Soon after arriving in India Rhys was asked to take a commission and even though he said yes he realised he could be posted to another regiment if he passed the officer training course (OTC). He asked his section officer if he could remain with the regiment. It was decided to leave it in abeyance until the course was finished. Rhys was told unofficially his request had been taken as far as the brigadier.

He was away three months and when he was told when he passed the course that he would remain with the regiment, but transferred to a different company as a second lieutenant, Rhys was more than pleased. He also had a small platoon of Ghurka soldiers under his command. Rhys would often say they were born fighters, but he never felt confident enough to turn his back on them.

In between spells of fighting Rhys again started to box for the regiment, but it was harder as the men knew he was an officer and they felt it was a question of pride and honour to beat an officer in the ring. He again became middleweight champion of the brigade. The regiment were proud of the honour he brought them. The conditions they fought under were appalling with dysentery, malaria and fighting against an enemy whose aim was to kill whatever the cost.

Rhys was promoted to first lieutenant and shortly afterwards came down with malaria, but he was not the exception as most of the regiment at one time or another came down with the complaint. However, he had a long spell in hospital with dysentery. Rhys returned home with the rank of captain in 1946 with his health ruined, but after some months his health did improve. He decided not to return to the colliery and took up employment as a maintenance fitter. He never declared to his employer he had been an officer and would say as the qualities his OC had seen were still there, there was no reason why he could not climb the promotion ladder again.

Rhys had terrible bouts of malaria which would come on without warning. One moment he would be talking and the next moment covered in perspiration and unable to stop shivering. If Glenys was there when an attack started she would get him into bed and telephone the doctor, describe the symptoms to him and say what she had done. The doctor knew Glenys had nursed soldiers from overseas and would then tell her if what she had done was correct. Glenys had a special relationship with Rhys who would readily allow her to minister to his health needs. He was always in pain and some discomfort, but if there were any signs of weakness due to this Glenys would be the only one who knew as there was complete trust between them.

Rhys had a lot to make up and the first two years after being demobbed were no fun, but he was beginning to enjoy his work and to his employers it would appear they realised he would be an asset to them and all those who came in contact with him could not but like him.

Rhys started to see a young girl named Gwen who worked in the local newspaper shop. She was two years younger than him. They first noticed each other when he called for his cigarettes each morning. It was soon evident they idolised each other, but as they both had strong characters there was little room for compromise if they had a difference of opinion. They became engaged very quickly and set the date for the wedding. Their wedding day was a well attended occasion with over seventy guests excluding the children. They spent the honeymoon a few miles away at a small hotel.

They eventually bought a house in the village, but it needed a lot done to it before they could move in. Rhys worked hard to make a proper home for Gwen and whenever any overtime was available he took it. He received promotion as a planner in the production department. The extra pay certainly helped them. It seemed no time before they had two children and both were pleased with their young family. Shortly afterwards he had a recurrence of his illness and had another medical board and his war disability pension was increased. The extra money was more than acceptable, but only confirmed he was not getting better. Gwen was the ideal wife as she protected him without Rhys knowing it. He loved to play with the children, but as his health declined he would soon tire.

Llewellyn would call and both would go out for a drink and talk about their apprenticeship days in the colliery and when Rhys was asked when assisting the fitter underground to fetch a left-handed spanner and after about an hour returned with a ten foot rail section weighing about a hundred weight, and it almost creased him, naturally they would talk about John in Australia. Somehow neither brought Gareth into the conversation.

It was strange how two brothers so different in appearance, with Gareth short and Rhys tall had so much in common. As soon as either smiled you knew they were brothers by an uncanny likeness. The shape of their mouths and teeth took on a transformation and their eyes would light up, and it was as if it was something special to them. Neither of them knew the meaning of the words 'to give in' or be afraid of anything or anyone and when Gareth was killed at Normandy something died in Rhys. The same could be said of Rhys, as he left too much of himself in Burma.

Rhys was the favourite of his mam and when he called in to see her there was a magic between them, not all that different as between him and Gareth. The three of them were cast in the same mould. God help her if anything happened to him. Rhys and his dad had a lot of respect for each other and were able to communicate without the need for words. Both were good listeners.

There was always the feeling his challenge was still to come and this unexplained part of him which could not be readily understood. It was almost as if he knew, and did not try to control the inevitable, and for a lesser man than Rhys the outcome would be less predictable. The feeling of uncertainty took on all sorts of forms, such as whether his family knew, and wanting to be over-protective towards him and at the same time keeping a secret of their knowledge to themselves. It was harder for Gwen as she saw him not only at his best, but also at his lowest ebb, when he most wanted support.

Rhys was still working his way up the promotion ladder and was offered the manager's position in the production department. He accepted the increased responsibility and additional work load. With his children growing up and having fewer demands on them Gwen and Rhys had more time together and were able to go out more.

When Rhys and Llewellyn went out for their occasional drink together on a Sunday morning Rhys would have a game of darts or cards and Llewellyn would sit and watch. Llewellyn tried not to look at Rhys and if at the same time Rhys would catch the look he gave one of his smiles as if to allay any worries Llewellyn had about him. His intuition on occasions seemed frightening. It was as if he knew exactly what Llewellyn was thinking and to tell him not to worry, and to say, 'I know you will help me over the hardest part, which is facing the end with dignity.'

His new promotion did little to improve his declining health and it was not long afterwards that he started going into hospital to see the specialist. On his way home from these visits he always called in to see his mam and dad. Going into the third and fourth year his visits to hospital became more frequent and he would stay for longer durations. When he went in he was exhausted, but looked great after the treatment. Llewellyn and Rhys still went for their Sunday morning drink, but Rhys was less inclined to play darts or cards.

By this time Avril was married and moved away from the village, but she very infrequently called in to see Rhys. Her husband Ivor never liked visiting sick people.

Their dad by this time was feeling out of sorts and shortly after went into hospital, without getting better, and died within two weeks. His death was a blow to the family as he was very knowledgeable, and any one of them going to him for advice were never disappointed with the answer.

On one of the occasions Llewellyn visited Rhys in the hospital he was in his pyjamas and dressing-gown, and started to talk about their younger days and when he would ask Llewellyn to call their mam to say there was no paper in the toilet, and it was the reference to that incident that made Llewellyn think Rhys may not have a lot of time left.

John had written from Australia and said they had decided to return home with the family for good and live in Scotland. About a month later there was a letter from Catherine to say John had died.

Rhys was at home when Llewellyn told him about John and looking him straight in the face he said, 'Rhys, don't give up, as it is not what John would want,' and it was the first time he had his guard down since his illness. Llewellyn wanted to hold him but he did not, and afterwards wished he had. Brothers are supposed to show their feelings sometimes.

When Rhys called to see his mam he could see that suddenly she looked old and he was reminded the end of the war only means the end of the fighting, but does not stop those dying from the results of the war and in the end the winners were losers when the cost in human lives has to be accounted for.

When Catherine returned home and went down to John's mam she had the same look on her face as their mam.

Over the next few years Rhys was spending longer periods in hospital than at home. Glenys would make at least two visits to see him and they always appeared to have plenty to say to each other, but Llewellyn was never part of the private chats they had. Rhys and Llewellyn developed a code of rules in their behaviour and conversation. If it was not so serious one could smile at the silliness of it all, especially as they both knew there was not a lot of time left for the one, but it became a question of pride with neither wanting to break the rules. The cost to Rhys to hide his pain and the inevitability of it at least gave him peace of mind, but what about the lying in bed in the darkness with only the thought of what was to come. The hospital staff were understanding because sometimes there were as many as ten visitors around his bed. Usually the relatives gave his friends preference when there were too many there.

Rhys had by now stopped going to work and after leaving the hospital after treatment would only go for short walks, and wherever he went Gwen would be with him. They were inseparable and the family would stay away. If ever two people needed their love it was them and both crammed into the period of his illness more love for each other than many who lived to be a hundred, and if there is a God he gave those two the opportunity to keep stock of their love.

Rhys only came home for one more stay and after he had been back there a few days Gwen rang Llewellyn and suggested he went to see Rhys no later than a few days. When he went in the next morning and Rhys asked what he was doing there so early, he said, 'I am going for an interview at 12.30 for a new job.' This was the one occasion both were thankful for the unofficial rules. They discussed the interview and how to get there. Rhys gave him detailed instructions on how to get there and how long it would take and he reminded Llewellyn of the occasion he said, 'Llewellyn is the brainy one.' By now if the rules were to be observed it was time to leave. Rhys looked at his watch and said, 'It's 12 o'clock.'

It was too late to change the rules and Llewellyn got up to leave and at that moment thought he was going to break down in front of him, and as Rhys grasped his hand he said, 'Hang on a little longer, Llewellyn,' but he could not stop the tears. The tears started to run down the face of Rhys, and with a final effort Rhys said, 'You'd better hurry or you will be late for your appointment.'

As Llewellyn stood up to say, 'So long until the next time,' they again gripped eath other's hands so tightly it hurt, but not as much as inside.

They looked at each other with eyes wet with tears, and Rhys said, 'Best of luck with the interview.'

As Llewellyn crossed the ward to the door he turned with a silent 'bless you', they waved at each other and when he sat in his car asked himself how anyone too young for war service deserved this. Yet Rhys accepted without anger. Rhys died that evening. This was how it was to be, Rhys knew it, and the family knew it, and did we prefer to keep a brave face and not express the true feelings, because in the end it would make no difference? Or was Rhys right to want it kept up to the end?

RHYS SAID TO LLEWELLYN,

'Tell Mam there is no paper in here.'

THE PARADE

The parade was finished for another year and even though the atmosphere of the occasion gave a person a lift to make it all worthwhile, and a reason to attend the next Remembrance parade and service, there was still the one enemy whom they could not fight against and expect to win – old age. One is reminded in the months between the next occasion when the Union Jack Flag flies at half-mast at some British Legion clubs to denote an ex-service person has died.

On the evening of the parade when the pomp and ceremony is over and one pays a visit to the Cenotaph and reads the cards on the wreaths that it is not only the Associations who attend but relatives of those who laid down their lives for Queen/King and Country.

TO THEIR DAD:

*'Old soldiers do die, but to Llewellyn
never fade away.'*

Epigraph

The Edwards' family story has portrayed the life of two people from entirely different environments who by their sheer hard work and against all odds survived the poverty which was with the family until after the middle thirties, and the improvements against those conditions were due to unemployment. Their dad's ill health on his return from the POW camp in Germany in 1919 made it difficult to hold down a job. Later on an accident at the colliery where he worked took four years before he was fit to hold down work. What was the point of fighting for his country from 1916 when it resulted in hardship and illness until his death? Their children were obliged to wear clothes given them and their mam had to work on the most menial tasks to provide them with food.

With the start of the Second World War the four eldest sons were called up in September 1939.

Mam and Dad

A few years after their dad died their mam decided to live with her oldest daughter and has now reached a very old age.

Glenys and Llewellyn

They lead a quiet life after the active years from the war and like most people growing older, tend to look back and not to the future.

Megan and Andrew

Andrew improved his education and made strides forward and became an equal partner in the furniture business. He was able to have the active support of Megan.

Avril and Ivor

They achieved monetary success and acceptance of their love for each other, but their collective contribution of the family dwindled as the years went by.

Sian and Phillip

They have a happy and contented marriage, with a nice home.

151

Owen and Jean

Their marriage was doomed from the beginning because Owen considered the pursuit of wealth above happiness, and it was Jean who suffered.

Ann and Gareth

She found her one and only partner in Gareth and in spite of their inability to get married they found in the end it did not make any difference to them as they were able to cram into four days what most can only achieve in a lifetime. The child born eight months after Gareth was killed in Normandy in 1944. Ann never married or gave any thought to anyone else as her love for Gareth remains with her, as she knows Gareth's does. Gareth knew when given embarkation leave he would not return and during his last leave bitterly regretted not marrying.

John and Catherine

The death of John was a loss Catherine took many years to recover from, but she eventually remarried someone from her home village. She makes her annual visits to the local Cenotaph with her wreath and during the service tightly holds the medals pinned to the lapel of her coat which John won during the war. Her husband who went with her to the service would watch over her and the warm smile she gave him made up for any love he thought he may not have from her.

Gwen and Rhys

Theirs was the story of two people whose love for each other enabled them to come to terms with the knowledge that the physical expression of their love can be exchanged for love which is not readily understandable to others, even knowing the short time they had left together. Gwen to this day is unable to understand how he was able to hide from her the nearness of the end until the end.

Llewellyn Edwards

Llewellyn decided to write the story of the family as he walked from the ward on the day Rhys died, and even then realised that when it was finished it was not the end until he knew the full cost had been assessed.

The Gulf War

The Gulf War, to service personnel of the Falklands War, can be looked upon in the same way as their war can be looked upon by those who served in earlier fields of operation such as Cyprus, Suez, Malaya, Korea, and Palestine, and further back to the Second World War, and the First World War. The only difference between these wars are the communications, techniques, and weaponry, and these are briefly decribed below;

- The First World War was semi-static trench warfare, with the other two Services playing a minor role to the Army.
- The Second World War fully integrated the three Services. The Army using tanks and infantry was extremely mobile.
- Palestine and Cyprus mainly involved the Army for policing duties.
- Malaya, Korea, and Suez relied on a concentration of infantry and tanks supported by the Royal Air Force.
- The Falklands War used highly specialist infantry supported by the other two Services.
- The Gulf War is applying newly tried and very sophisticated computer controlled weapons with the Royal Air Force being the main Service supported by the Army, and the Navy.

The weaponry difference between the First World War and the Gulf War is so obvious that it is frightening. It is certainly a change to go from rifles, machine guns and artillery to missiles; with a single item of warfare costing twelve million pounds or a missile one million pounds they are a more effective method of killing and maiming, or are they?

In spite of the fact that those conducting the progress of the war appear to be more knowledgeable by the use of computer controlled intelligence feeding back information, there is still the one feature which remains the same whatever war is fought. This is that *nothing happens until the well-trained soldier, sailor, airman pulls the trigger, presses the switch or steers the warship..*

When the casualties start and the telegrams or other means inform the next of kin, the same apprehension and worries of the relatives are still there, and always have been. Irrespective of how a war is started and fought the headstone above the grave at any war grave cemetery gives the same information whatever the period or war.

Politicians should be reminded of this when they start a war, as it is most unlikely you will see their names on any war grave headstone, and when reassuring words are uttered by them saying right is on our side or it is a war to end war, it is no consolation to the casualties.

Our religious leaders are equally forthcoming when they say God is on our side, and so are the religious leaders of our enemy who will say God is on their side, so God is on both sides, in the same way that right is on both sides.

The *Chink Of Medals* story reveals how the family of service personnel copes with the grief when their loved ones are killed or suffer appalling injuries. Even those who come home unscathed, or apparently so to the outsider, are never quite the same.

Llewellyn Edwards.